THE HOMELESS
HEART-THROB

Crystal Jeans

HONNO MODERN FICTION

First published in 2019 by Honno Press, 'Ailsa Craig', Heol y Cawl,
Dinas Powys, Vale of Glamorgan, Wales, CF64 4AH

1 2 3 4 5 6 7 8 9 10

A catalogue record for this book is available from the British Library.

Published with the financial support of the Welsh Books Council.

ISBN 978-1-912905-01-0 (paperback)
ISBN 978-1-912905-02-1 (ebook)

Cover design: Annika Faircloth
Cover illustration: Ben Faircloth
Text design: Elaine Sharples
Printed in Great Britain by 4edge

THE HOMELESS HEART-THROB

To Mum and Dad

Acknowledgements

A version of Japanese Flag first published in Fuck the Rules, Leviathan, 2017

A version of My Bukowski first published in New Welsh Reader 109, autumn 2015, https://newwelshreview.com/article.php?id=1054

A version of Split Me in Two, Gareth Moon first published in New Welsh Review 104, spring 2014, https://newwelshreview.com/article.php?id=683

With thanks for permission to reprint lyrics
"First Time Ever I Saw Your Face"
Written by Ewan Maccoll
Published by Harmony Music LTD, Roundhouse,
212 Regents Park Road Entrance, London NW1 8AW

Thank you to all the tutors and students on my MPhil at the University of South Wales for their helpful critiques on some of these chapters. Thanks to the team at Honno for, yet again, taking the chance (especially Caroline Oakley) and also Gwen Davies and David Owain Hughes for publishing earlier versions of these chapters. Thanks to all the real-life people whose characteristics and general auras I've poached for my own artistic self-interest. Thanks to Pauline and Rod. Special thanks to Hannah Austin for her editorial help. Cheers to Molly. And lastly, thanks to Renn for being lush.

Contents

Split Me in Two, Gareth Moon

2007

He asks me if I keep a diary still.

'God no. No. I don't know why I kept one at all.'

It had been the child psychologist's idea. But I'd never tell him that.

Dennis shifts the tobacco around the Rizla with a black fingernail. He sprinkles some twiggy skunk over the top, his jaw slack. 'I had a look at some of mine the other day,' he says, rolling the deck into a tampon and licking it shut. 'I looked at the one from when we were fourteen.' He closes his eyes and slowly shakes his head. 'So fucking embarrassing.'

'What's so embarrassing?'

'That crush I had on Gareth Moon. Remember? I won't go into details, what with you being a repressed fag in denial, but God, the filth that went through my mind!' He shakes his head again, this time in disbelief. 'Pass me that whisky, would you, Kev?'

I pass it. (I like the way it sloshes like a full stomach when he tilts it to his lips.)

'And it all went in the fucking diary. Every time my heart fluttered for him. Every wank, practically. And I drew these little pictures too, these diagrams of what I wanted him to do to me.'

'Lovely.'

'And, uch, it wasn't just sexual. I actually thought I loved him. *Loved* him.'

1

'You cried about him once.'

'I know! Because that dick from art class, what was his name?' A click of his fingers. 'Joseph. Fucking Joseph Parsons. He said he saw Penny Small wanking Gareth off in the park. That killed me. And I used to write in my diary, I used to write, "I love him so much I'd die for him." And my name with his surname. "Dennis Moon." To see how it would look on paper.'

'That's really not that embarrassing. Really.' I'm thinking of my own diary, about the blood staining April.

'It is though. And those diagrams! God. There's this one picture, yeah? – Oh, it's *awful* – there's this one picture, drawn in red Biro. And in it he's doing me, you know, up the—'

'Yes, OK,' I say.

'It's practically stick figures it's so bad, but the cock and balls, oh! I did the cock and balls in real detail. Like, *veiny* detail, you know? With moisture clinging like dewdrops and wrinkles in the ball sack. And that seam – you know that seam? On the balls? That much detail. And little squiggles and lines to represent movement. Like you get in *The Beano*. And there's a speech bubble coming out of my mouth, saying – this is so *awful* – saying, "Split me in two!"' He shakes his head again, but there's a smile on his lips.

We don't speak for a while. Dennis takes this time to drain the bottle. Which I paid for. I remember how he deliberately cultivated a taste for whisky back when we were younger because he thought it would impress straight men. He drops the bottle over the side of the bed and it falls on to the edge of a loaded ashtray, catapulting ash and butts onto the bedroom floor. Dennis' bedroom is an assault course of fag ends, clothes, dirty socks, empty lager and cider cans, vodka and whisky bottles, and carrier bags of sick. The bed he's lying on, stretched out like an Egyptian princess, has probably been pissed on at least twice this week.

'Why don't you burn them all then?' I finally say.

'Uh?'

'The diaries,' I say.

'Burn them? Would you burn yours?'

I think about it. 'No.'

'But have you ever thought about what happens to them when we die?'

'I don't know.' I stretch my back, roll my neck. I've been crouched over my crossed legs for three or more hours now.

'Think about it.' Dennis stretches his arm out to me and flaps his hand impatiently. I pass him the spliff. 'Imagine you die and your mum reads it. She's not gunna like hearing about all those old ladies you raped, is she?'

'Oh, ha ha, fuck off. My diary was quite boring, actually.' This isn't true. My diary was psychotic. Until they plied me with the anti-psychotics. Then it evolved into morbidity.

'Did it have sexual diagrams?' he asks.

'Yep. Lots of tit pictures. Nice shading.' Another lie. I was practically asexual when I was fourteen. The anti-psychotics and anti-depressants. The 'calmers'. My dick was about as useful as the school psychologist.

'You know what we should do?' I say.

'Make love,' he says.

'Shut up. Seriously.'

'What?'

'We should make a deal. If I die, you burn my diaries for me. And vice versa.'

Dennis thinks about it. He opens his mouth in a tight-lipped 'O' with the gormless distraction of a woman putting on eyeliner, and scratches the corner of his lips with his little finger. 'That's actually a brilliant idea.'

'Deal, then?'

'Yes.'

'Where do you keep them?' I say.

'Under the bed.'

'Mine are in my underwear drawer. Don't fucking read them.' I'm about to suggest we shake on it but I remember Dennis once admitting that he never washes his hands.

I get the phone call on a Sunday morning. I'm busy shaving off the copper frizz that grows on my chin like mould. 'Yeah?' I say, dripping foam onto my T-shirt.

Silence. No, not quite; a quiet gurgling noise.

'Who is it?'

'Hello? Kevin?' Soft-spoken, Scottish accent. Dennis's mum.

'Oh hiya, Mrs McClune.'

'Hi. Kevin. Sorry, I – I. Give me a second.' The trumpet honk of a nose being blown. 'Sorry. Kevin. Um. God. It's bad news.'

And without even thinking, I say: 'He's dead, isn't he?'

Silence.

'Mrs – Pam, *tell* me?' My voice feels and sounds wooshy and far away, like it's coming out of a seashell.

'Dead. He's dead. Silly bastard.' A groan. 'He was drinking – you know how drunk he could get. Silly wee bastard – I always said, I always said – Oh, I can't *do* this!'

Dead.

'He fell down the stairs, Kevin! I found him at the bottom of the stairs at six o'clock this morning, and his neck was bent like a – like a, I don't know, it was almost a ninety-degree angle. Can you imagine that?' A long, deep groan, tailing off into a wail. 'I could see' – this in a ghoulish whisper – 'I could see his vertebrae pushing through the

4

skin of his neck. Oh God. Oh God. I'm sorry, Kevin. I need to go.'

I hear the phone click. I swallow slowly and dryly.

I feel nothing. Nothing.

I only have one nice suit and it's not even nice. Black, thin grey pin stripes, mauve shirt, my gut underneath it strains against the buttons. I bought it three years ago in H&M. Job interview with BT. Never got the job. Sprayed some Febreeze into the armpits, put it back in my wardrobe for future failures. Didn't think I'd ever have to wear it to look at a dead body and go to a funeral.

Dennis would've wanted me to Goth up. He loved my Robert Smith phase. But at funerals you're not there for the deceased; you're there for the ones left alive. I'm here for Mrs. McClune. With the long, thick salt and pepper hair and pretty brown eyes. Pam. Who invited me to Sunday roasts because my own mother has MS and can't do much. Who brought me a glass of cold orange juice – with bits in – on the mornings I slept over. Who kissed me once, in the kitchen, sloppily and desperately, and then drew away quickly, and never spoke of it again.

'I can't do this alone,' she says, grabbing my cold hand and pulling me along with her. I don't want to see the body. Not because I'm afraid of crying but because I'm afraid of not crying.

Dennis looks like a fat vampire. His hands are folded over his stomach as if he's dozing after a big meal. He looks younger than twenty-seven. They've shaved him, which is a shame because thick stubble helped to hide his chubby jaw line. And they've cleaned the black nail varnish off. I bet Pam wants it that way. Pam wants her boy clean.

Pam is standing very still. Just looking. She leans over his

5

body and kisses his paper-white forehead, stroking the side of his face with such tenderness, like he's a sleeping child.

The seats are mostly empty – alcoholics tend to lose a lot of friends. And Dennis could be an arsehole sometimes. Everything here is pine – the floor, the podium, the coffin. The artificial lighting is horrible. I take a seat next to Pam, close my eyes and let the service wash over me. *Dennis was a creative soul, a happy spirit. Dennis always looked out for his common man, Dennis loved people.* Lies.

A few lines from Matthew. A story about a shepherd and his flock. Something about Jesus, about Dennis being wrapped warm and safe by the loving arms of Jesus. I wonder what Jesus thought about that Cradle of Filth hoody Dennis used to wear. 'Jesus is a Cunt.' I hope Jesus is in a forgiving mood. The priest, a red-faced man with black wiry eyebrows, presses play on the CD player behind him – a recorded hymn. *Abide with me.*

Two shiny-suited men wheel the coffin behind a maroon curtain. Will he go straight to the crem now? I don't know how these things work. I wonder what burning flesh smells like – chicken? Pork? Do fat corpses take longer? The priest thanks us all for coming. That's it then. Pamela snorts back some snot and takes my arm. She forces a smile. 'Come on, let's go to the pub.'

'I could do with a drink,' I say.

'*A* drink? This is Dennis's day. We might as well get trollied.' She gives me a dig in the ribs and I laugh. 'Nice to see you show some emotion. You're still in shock, aren't you?'

I nod. Yes, I'm in shock. That's what it must be.

*

6

The Golden Cross is a gay pub frequented by old queens and plump lesbians in polo shirts. Dennis hated the place and only went along now and then for disastrous karaoke and drag shows.

I chat with Lou and Polly, a couple of lesbians who live on the end of Tarleton Avenue – Dennis's street. They'd once invited Dennis over for dinner and he'd ended up calling Polly a fat ugly dyke then puking in their hallway. Lou had been friends with Dennis before she got with Polly. They'd had a mutually destructive friendship based on drink and drugs; too many ugly nights ending in blackouts. Lou even punched him once, splitting his lip so badly that he had to take his piercing out. They didn't talk for ages, but then, last year, Lou reached out to him with the dinner invite, maybe to avoid the awkwardness of bumping into each other in the street. Or maybe she still cared about him. But I guess deep down he was still sore over the split lip. 'You're a fucking hypocrite,' he apparently said to her, after she expressed concern over his drinking, 'and your girlfriend's a fat ugly dyke, lol.' I can imagine him saying it, a sly, mean humour in his eyes. That 'lol' at the end. But here they are, showing their respects, shaking their heads sadly.

It's cleansing, death.

Pamela thanks them for coming. She finds Deena, a beautiful Indian woman with thick eyeliner and lots of piercings who also lives in Tarleton Avenue (next door to the lesbians) and who went to school with Dennis, and later, university. She was another old drug buddy. Last I heard she'd argued with Dennis – called him a narcissistic twat apparently (Dennis: 'Like *she* can talk.') – and blocked him on Facebook. It couldn't have been easy for him, living in a street surrounded by old friends who didn't like him anymore. Dennis seethed at the idea that those 'dykes' and that 'fag hag' were living next door to each other. 'Probably get together and read me to filth,' he'd say. 'In between scissoring each other.' A nauseous shudder.

I wait until Deena and Pamela are stuck in conversation. I down my drink and go.

I've known about the key in the plant pot for a long time. Pamela trusts me. The homeless man who bums around this area is sat on a wall across the street. Dennis used to pretend to fancy him just to gross me out; he called him Monsterberry Crush for no explicable reason – he was always coming up with irreverent nicknames for people. Monsterberry Crush is looking down at his hands, making a roll-up. I fish the key out and open the door. The burglar alarm emits a series of beeps so I push in the four-digit number to stop it.

I take my shoes off at the bottom of the stairs because it's a nice middleclass house with nice cream carpets (Dennis's dad – deceased now – had been a lawyer), but then I get to Dennis' room and it's like an infected boil on a supermodel's arse cheek. The purple walls are covered in old, drooping posters – Nine Inch Nails, Marilyn Manson, an out of place Take That for ironic value. The bed is covered in clothes, crusty dinner plates, and the dirty white pillow is splashed with a large purple stain. Cans of Strongbow and two bottles of Robinson's blackcurrant line up along the bed. There's his favourite cup – the black resin goblet covered in little skulls. Still half full.

This is the death room, undisturbed. It tells a story: Dennis is up here alone drinking cider and black. He vomits on his pillow, says 'oh, no' in that Phoebe Buffay way. Later he gets hungry, fancies a tube of Pringles and a packet of Jaffa Cakes. Goes downstairs. Trips on the stairs. Tumbles, flips, snaps his neck…

8

I sit down. Heart's beating a bit fast. Dangerous sign. I find the Valium, the blessed Valium, in my breast pocket and dry-swallow five. Just to be safe. I crawl over the lumpy terrain of the floor toward the bed and there it is underneath, the box of diaries – three books, all of them covered in doodles and stickers from *Smash Hits* and *Kerrang*.

I want to see that sketch of Dennis being bumfucked by Gareth Moon.

It's in the second book and it's exactly like Dennis described it. A three-year-old could've drawn the bodies and faces, but the genitals are pure art. And there's the speech bubble: 'Split me in two!'

I rip the page out of the book, fold it up, stuff it into my breast pocket.

Dennis has a fireplace in his room, the mantelpiece topped with black skulls and candles stuffed into wine bottles. Pamela told him that the chimney was blocked and it couldn't be used – a lie. 'I'm not letting that silly wee pisshead burn the house down,' she once told me over a chopping board of onions.

It takes a while to get the fire going because the Vals are starting to take effect – fifty milligrams on an empty stomach. After five pints at the reception. But soon it's raging and my face feels tight like Cling Film. I drop the diaries one at a time into the fire from between pinched fingers, like I'm feeding fish heads to a shark. I open the window to let out the smoke and sit on the floor. The paper shrinks, curls, blackens. It's nice; the warmth, the gentle crackling noises. I could get cosy here.

Dennis was eaten by flames today, I think, and now his memories.

I'll do my best to remember what I can for him.

The time he got his knob pierced and passed out, holding my hand. The time he ate so much Toblerone he got sick and had to miss the Trivium gig. The time he went to AA, pissed, and told them they were all self-righteous cunts. The time he—

'Fuck. How the – shit.' I spring into the air fast, as if I'm not five stone overweight. Fire's spilled – a trail of flickering flames leading from the grate to a pile of clothes on the floor. Pants, black combats, T-shirts. There's paper too, chip shop paper, unopened T-Mobile bills, a couple of *Metal Hammer*s. The fire curls its tongue around the edge of the heap and I'm just standing there like some anxious ghoul, watching.

I need to stamp it out but I left my shoes downstairs. Fuck. I see Dennis's boots, the giant New Rocks he got for Christmas when he was twenty-two. Knee-high, metal everywhere, dull silver flames emblazoned along the sides. I crouch, grunting over my waistband, and slip my feet into the boots. They're at least five sizes bigger than my own. I concentrate on one small patch, stamping over and over. Don't heroes put out fires?

Don't idiots start them?

I'm all adrenaline. Black smoke up my nose, in my eyes. And then one of the boots flies off and bangs against the wardrobe. I go and get it, push my foot back in. Twenty seconds – that's all it takes for the bits of fire I've stamped out to start up again.

And here comes the panic. Jagged slivers tearing through the Diazepam calm – a blade slitting a goose-feather pillow. I grab Dennis's stinky quilt and throw it over the fire. It misses, falls short, fans the flames. Fuck. I try again. It lands and I jump on the duvet and stomp around like Yosemite Sam.

It works. Jesus, it works. Jesus, you are not a cunt. I peek under the duvet. Black rags and smoky ashes. A dark circle. I stumble out of the room, still wearing Dennis's boots. I clobber down the stairs and launch my way out of the house. I land sprawling on the fresh clean turf outside, dizzy, sick, everything pulsating. You can't explain a panic attack to someone who's never experienced it except by saying you'd rather die. And that's ironic, because the panic comes from thinking you're going to die.

I raise myself up, breathing deep. I slap a hand to my chest to feel my heartbeat (always a mistake). My fingers brush the piece of paper I tore from the diary; it's poking out of the top of my breast pocket. I pull it out, clutch it in my clammy hands. Breathe, breathe, breathe, slowly. There's Monsterberry Crush, still sitting on the wall, bottle of cider on his thigh, a blue carrier bag by his feet. Dennis used to sing this song about him. He'd sing it along to the Gummi Berry Juice song from the eighties Gummi Bears cartoon. *Monsterberry, Monsterberry Crush/Monsterberry, Monsterberry Crush...*

Monsterberry Crush tips his flagon in my direction. He has a ginger beard and looks happier than he has a right to be. *Monsterberry, Monsterberry Crush/Monsterberry, I've only got one wish...* There was a bit that came after that, something about drinking his cum with a tablespoon, something revolting – no, a ladle, drinking it with a ladle. *With a ladle, drink it cuz it's lush/it's Monsterberry Crush—*

And my face buckles like a crashed car and I start crying. The street becomes a glistening blur.

My Bukowski

There's this homeless guy. He must be around fifty. He hangs out in the lanes behind Tamerlane Road, by the allotments. He's always wearing a pair of jeans and a leather jacket. He has light red hair, turning grey, a beard. Old scars and pits on his face, skin rough and red. Dirty. He looks really dirty. I see him when I'm walking my dog. He's always got a flagon of cider. Sometimes he's sitting on the floor outside someone's garage, other times just ambling along. He nods at me, tips his head, a silent hi.

There's something in his eyes that I like.

The first time I saw him I was walking the dog with my ten-year-old daughter. We passed through the allotments and got onto the lane that runs along the dual carriageway, and there he was. Slumped against a tree trunk, out of it, dirty hands loosely cupping a bottle of cider – Country Choice. He'd pissed himself. Crotch like a dark continent.

My daughter looked confused. 'Is he asleep?'

'Yes.'

'He's peed himself.'

'He has.'

I kicked his boot and he opened his eyes.

'You're going to freeze,' I said.

He nodded and slowly stood up, squinting at my dog. After a few seconds I looked back and he was gone.

*

12

I'm on all fours, palms and knees sinking into the soft duvet. And I suddenly imagine that it's him. *Him.* My husband speeds up and says, 'Yeah. Yeah,' through clenched teeth and I imagine that they're *his* words. The hands cupping my pelvis are *his* hands with the black finger creases.

Afterwards, the husband smiles and says, 'You seemed to enjoy yourself.' I snuggle into his neck and can almost smell alcohol, old sweat and cigarettes infused in a leather jacket.

Associations. I've been making associations. Tramp equals filth. Therefore I want some filth. Germs, grime, bad smells, impurity. A rebellion? But aren't I rebelling enough, with the occasional three-ways and the S&M?

A class thing? I wouldn't put it past myself. Low self-esteem? Doubtful. Something from my childhood? Like, once I saw my mum blowing my dad in the kitchen while I hid next to the overflowing bin, except I pushed it down deep and only now has my psyche decided to retch it up.

A simple fetish? Maybe I'm like Napoleon, who apparently sent a letter to his wife saying, 'Dear Josephine, I will be arriving home in three days. Don't bathe.'

I just don't know. A strange craving – pickled eggs from the jar – maybe that's all it is.

And that look he gives me, it's a sort of charm. A confidence. Like he could have me.

The daughter is arranging my bookcase alphabetically. I swear she's going to grow up to be obsessive compulsive. Or a librarian. She brings a book over. *Women*, by Charles Bukowski. 'It's all broken,' she says. 'Look.' A bunch of pages fall out. 'You should throw it away, Mum.'

'Pass it here.'

I pick up the fallen pages and slot them back in. I notice

a black and white profile shot of the author on the inside cover and ping! goes the lightbulb.

I started out reading Bukowski for an essay in uni. The usual feminist shtick about his objectification of women. I was supposed to hate this man. In his earlier books he's a down-and-out bum, a low-life, who drifts from menial job to menial job. At the time of *Women*, he's a misanthropic old writer who likes drinking whisky, gambling and fucking woman after woman – many of them young and pretty. He's an ugly old bastard too – lumpy, acne-blasted face, monkey mouth, eyes like slits.

I wanted to be one of his women, to go over his cheap LA apartment in a yellow dress and have him scooch up to me on the couch and run his gorilla hands up my bare legs and breathe his whisky-stink into my face. To screw me, badly. Selfishly. It couldn't be good. But I'd still go back for more. I'd make him love me. He'd write poems about me. The Welsh girl he met on tour who fucked him with earthy abandon and never said no to anal.

I flip the pages of *Women* and read random pages, smiling. And I look at the picture again.

Lately I've been avoiding the lanes by the allotments because the crazy old Irish bitch who feeds the stray cats has started throwing apples at my dog. But I want to see my Bukowski.

One morning I see them both. Crazy Cat Lady's pouring dry cat food into an old margarine tub. Four cats sit around watching her. They see my lolloping Beagle and run like hell. Crazy Cat Lady looks up, eyes scrunched into evil lemon slices.

'Get dat dog away from here!'

'It's a lane,' I say. 'It's public proper—'

'You shut yer mouth and keep movin'.'

I keep moving.

'Dat's roight,' she yells, 'keep on walkin'. Do not pass go, do not collect two haundred pounds.'

And then I hear another voice. 'Oh no you don't.' A man's voice. Scratchy and smoke-grazed. My Bukowski.

My heart twists like a cold flannel. He's stood there, swaying and glaring at Crazy Cat Lady, who is on tiptoes picking a small red apple from the tree that overhangs the allotment fence.

She scowls at him. 'Oh, geddaway widja, ya vagrant.'

He shows her his flagon. 'You throw that at her, I'll throw this over you.' He tries to fix his bleary eyes on hers. 'Understand?'

'You wanna get a job, ya worthless fool.'

He takes a step forward.

'No, it's OK,' I say, rushing forward. 'Her aim's not very good. Honestly, it's fine.'

'You wanna get yerself an education!' she shouts at me. But she drops the apple. It lands on the floor and rolls into a pothole. She tuts with disgust and goes back into her garden.

I'm left alone with my Bukowski.

'Thanks,' I say.

He waves a hand. Black crescent moons under his nails. 'No worries, love.' He pulls a half-smoked roll-up out of his pocket. 'Gotta light?'

I lean in and light it for him. He cups his grainy hands around my own and sucks until the black ash frazzles red. I smell leather and a perfumey tang of ethanol, ashtrays and mouthwash. A pub smell. He gets on his knees and scratches my dog behind the ears. 'Hello, little fella, what's yer name?'

'Hank,' I say.

'Hank! That's a good, strong name.' He stands back up, almost falling over.

'Well I should be getting home,' I say.

He winks. 'Be seein' you.'

I walk away. I hope he's checking out my arse, Bukowski style.

We've argued, me and the husband. Because he wants to open up our relationship beyond the odd threesome and maybe sleep with other people. Separately.

I kicked him out of the house last Monday and he went to stay with his mother in Pontcanna, taking the dog with him. Now it's Thursday. I've been pacing the house, chain-smoking. Listening to Fleetwood Mac over and over. The daughter's in school. I pour myself a glass of some Fairtrade Pinot Noir my husband likes. The arsehole can't even pronounce it properly. Peenoh noor, he says. Arsehole. He's already got some woman lined up for himself, I think. That's why he's doing this. The arsehole. I get through the bottle and open another.

By lunchtime I'm hunting the lanes. It's a whim. Crazy. He won't be around and I'll go home and try and sober up. But I find him. Sitting on a fly-tipped car tyre, drinking.

'Hey, how's Hank?' he says.

'You remembered.'

He holds his hand out as if indicating a short child. 'Little brown and white fucker, this high.'

I pull two cigarettes out of my packet. 'Come with me.'

He sits with his legs open, bottle of my husband's IPA on his thigh. Relaxed. The old dog.

I'm wearing a short yellow dress and I've put on some Chopin, which is how it's supposed to go. He takes regular hits on his beer and looks around the room with drunken eyes that sometimes settle on my bare legs. Which is how it's supposed to go.

'Do you ever get into fights?' I ask him.

'Do I ever get into fights?'

'Hmm.'

'No I don't. I keep away from fights. People hit me sometimes.'

'Do they?'

'Yeah. Teenagers. When I've taken too much drink.'

'Can you take a punch?'

'I'm alive, aren't I?'

I throw him a cigarette. 'Do you work?'

'Used to.'

'What did you do?'

'Oh, this and that. Was a mechanic once – MOT tester. Used to sing a fair bit – I had some good pipes on me, way back when. Did some wedding gigs.'

'Can I do your hair?' I say.

'What?'

'Let me do your hair. Let me comb it.'

'You do whatever you like, love.'

I go get my comb then sit on his lap. His hair is all raggy around his face. Centre-parted, receding slightly. I comb it back. He squints up at me, smoke drifting out of his nose. He smells bad. I push some stray hairs behind his ears. 'That's better.' He has a scruffy widow's peak now. Hair pushed back, a little wavy at the rear. Like you-know-who.

He's standing on the bed in his off-white boxers, a cigarette dangling from his mouth, a copy of Bukowski's poetry in one hand, a bottle of beer in the other.

'"I got in the shower and burned my balls last Wednesday—"'

17

'No,' I say, splashing wine on my thighs. 'Do an American accent.'

He sucks on his cigarette and starts again. '"I got in the shower—"'

'Yes, like that. That's good. But more…gritty. You're tired of life, you hate people. Slow it down.'

'"I got in the shower –"' he glances at me, I nod '"– and burned my balls last Wednesday."' He takes a swig of beer. Sniffs. '"Met this painter called Spain. No, he was a cartoonist, well, I met him at a party."' He goes on reading nice and slow, smoking and drinking between lines, dropping ash on the bed. The accent comes and goes.

'"I not only burnt my balls in that shower last Wednesday, I spun around to get out of the burning water and burnt my bunghole too."'

He looks down at me. 'That isn't poetry. What kind of poetry is that?'

'That's a good attitude to have,' I say. 'But you're wrong. He's a genius.'

'It's stupid.'

I wave his comment away. 'Come down from there.' I go in my knicker drawer and pull out a condom. Bukowski wouldn't use a condom. But you can take something too far.

I push him off me. We lie there, breathing through our mouths. I have my forearm over my eyes. The clock in the hallway chimes three times. The daughter will be home soon.

'Sorry,' he says. 'I'm too drunk.'

'It's OK,' I say.

'Can I bum another smoke?' he says, in an American accent.

*

18

I see him off. I give him three pairs of my husband's boxers, a tuna sandwich and a dusty bottle of Drambuie left over from two Christmases ago.

'Till next time,' he calls, opening the small gate.

I watch him turn right – towards the lanes probably.

Then my daughter is turning in, her eyes on his retreating figure. She walks up the path in her blue school uniform. 'Mum?' she says, big eyes. 'That was the man who peed himself.'

I down the rest of my wine and stuff the empty bottle in the privet hedge. 'Yes, it was. The very man.'

The Last Day of The Sunshine

2006

When the girl fell through the sky the sun hit her piercing in a blaze of white light, looking for a moment like a star to wish on.

Estela noticed this just before her mind emptied of thoughts and the garden shears dropped out of her hand and Frida screamed from the trampoline.

One year ago, Estela placed a plate of grilled fish and vegetables in front of Frida and said, 'Eat.'

Frida looked down at the food coolly, as if it was a list of statistics, and picked up her fork. 'I don't like the skin,' she said.

'Then don't eat it.'

'Can I give it to Trog?'

'When you've finished.'

Estela sat on the back doorstep and lit a cigarette. The sun was high in the sky. No clouds. She closed her eyes as she smoked and saw red through her eyelids.

'Mum, aren't you eating?' said Frida through a mouthful of carrot.

'No. I'm not very hungry today.'

She saw Trog running along the top of the fence, smooth as a soundwave. He jumped onto the patio and approached her, his acid-yellow eyes looking into her own.

'*Hola*, my little shit.' She craned her neck to look into the kitchen. 'He's come for your fish, Fri.'

'Tell him he must wait,' said the little girl.

'Tell him yourself.'

'You must wait, Trog!'

Estela blew smoke into the cat's face, laughing when it jerked its head and ran away. She closed her eyes again, smoking her cigarette slowly.

She heard voices and opened her eyes. There was a man in the garden next door. A portly, middle-aged Asian. He was walking down the garden path toward the garage, carrying a large biscuit-brown cardboard box and squinting miserably against the sunlight. Every few steps he'd hoist the heavy box into a more comfortable position.

The man stopped when he noticed Estela. He put the box down, wiped sweat off his forehead and grinned. 'Hello.' He approached the fence and held out his hand. 'Or, hello, *neighbour*, I should say.'

She took his moist hand and squeezed it. 'I didn't know anyone was moving in.'

'Mizanur Chaudry. Call me Miz.'

His face was big and doughy. He was totally bald except for a neat wedge of black hair atop each ear. His lips were large and rubbery and so smooth she wanted to touch them. He had a thick moustache.

'Estela,' she said, a tight smile on her lips, 'Estela Moreno. Please, anything you need let me or my husband know.'

It was important he know that she had a husband.

'Thank you. Maybe you can tell me about the best shops and restaurants in this area? Things like that.'

There was movement high up. The windows of next door's attic room had ripped open and a girl of university age looked out. Estela couldn't make out her features. She had long black hair and various piercings, which flashed in the sun.

21

'Dad!' she yelled. 'There's mouse shit on the carpet!'

Scowling, Miz yelled back, in his own language.

The girl huffed, her shoulders dropping, and snatched herself away from the window.

'My daughter,' said Miz.

Estela smiled.

A brief silence.

'There are some good shops here,' she said. 'Some nice restaurants too. There's a...' She gaped up at him; she'd been about to recommend an Indian restaurant, Panama, where she often went with Cristián (their paneer was perfection), but perhaps that would come across ignorant. Like something a white person would say. 'There's a new pizza place that I like. Lots of cafés, too.'

'Yes?'

'Yes.' She laughed nervously. She didn't know what else to say.

'Well, that's good to hear.' Miz bent down and picked up the box. 'Very nice meeting you. *Neighbour.*' A weak laugh blustered out from under his fat moustache. He staggered away. Estela noticed the top of his hairy arse peeking out of his dishevelled slacks. She wondered if Cristián would end up like that in thirty years' time.

'Trog!'

Frida was at the doorway holding out a silver rag of fish skin. 'Trog, I have fish!'

'Leave it in his bowl,' said Estela. She lit a fresh cigarette from the dying butt of the last one, which she flicked into the drain.

'Fishy, fishy, fishy!'

'I said leave it in the bowl, Freedee. And go wash your hands and face.'

The small girl ran back in the house.

Estela looked up at next door's attic room, shielding her eyes from the sun. She saw a blur at the corner of the window. She quickly looked away.

Estela put her feet on the table. The radio was on – 'Kashmir' by Led Zeppelin. She flexed her leg to the beat and looked around the living room distractedly. Bored. It was always the same at this time of day.

Cristián came in, a burgundy towel wrapped around his waist, dark hair dripping water down his face and neck.

'Why are you smoking in here?' he asked, in Spanish.

'Because I want to.'

'What about Frida?'

'Fuck off, Cristián, she's not even in the room.'

'Estela.'

She stared at the fireplace.

'Estela.'

'Oh, for Christ's sake, Cristián!' She pulled her feet off the table and brought them to the wooden floor with a thud. 'I had my whole fucking family breathing their dirty Ducados in my face, and look at me, I'm fine.'

'Political correctness gone mad, eh?' he said, putting on an English accent.

'Well…yes actually.'

Laughing, he walked up to her. 'You look very nice today.'

'Don't be silly.' She was wearing denim hot pants smeared with old paint and a yellow halter top. 'These are my lazy clothes.'

He crouched down and squeezed her knee. 'So? Very nice all the same.' He moved in closer, kissing her softly on the lips. Then he snatched the cigarette out of her hand and ran across the room. He opened the window and flicked it out.

'You fucking faggot, Cristián!'

He walked out of the room, smiling broadly.

The following day she saw the girl from next door. She was hanging washing out on the line. Duvet covers, pillow-cases, sheets.

Estela was sitting on top of a disused rabbit hutch left by the previous tenants. She watched the girl from behind her sunglasses as she smoked.

She was older than Estela had first guessed – not so much university age as mid-twenties. She had perfectly-arched eyebrows and thick black hair piled on top of her head. She was one of those punks, like the kids who hung around near the Font de Sant Llorenç in Lleida. She used to pass them on her way home from school, embarrassed by her uniform and her mother. The girl's nose was pierced twice on one side, and her lip was pierced near the left hand corner. She had a cluster of stars tattooed on the inside of her wrist. Estela hadn't known you could get Indian punks. Well, she thought, why not?

An older woman came out into the garden. She was stout and pale and dressed in a gold and purple salwar kameez. Estela knew they were named so because she had befriended an Indian mother at toddler playgroup back when Frida was two. She'd thought it a lovely, silky word. *Salwar kameez.*

'You're doing it wrong,' said the older woman.

'Wha?' said the girl, squinting.

'*Paanch* pegs. *Paanch.*'

'Does it matter?'

'If the wind is blowing then bloody yes.'

The girl curled her lip. She snatched some pegs from her belt and snapped them onto the hanging bed linen.

The older woman watched her for a while, her eyes hard, and walked away.

'Mum,' the girl called.

'*Haan?*'

'Don't leave me any tea. I'm going over Den's tonight.'

'Is that wise?'

The girl rolled her eyes, muttering something. The woman went back in the house.

Estela continued to watch. She pointed her head down at her feet, or towards the greenhouse, but always her eyes were on the girl. At one point the girl glanced over. Her eyes met Estela's, through the sunglasses, and flickered back to the green and brown striped pillowcase under her chin.

Estela wondered if maybe her sunglasses weren't as dark as she'd originally thought.

She stubbed out her cigarette and slipped inside.

It was another week before Estela saw the girl again. She and Frida were eating their breakfast on the patio. The sun was high in the sky and blazing already.

The girl walked past the fence. She had one towel twisted around her hair, another wrapped around her body from the armpits down. She was on the phone.

'I don't think I'm overdrawn... Yeah.'

'Who is that lady?' asked Frida in a loud voice.

'Shhh. Eat your breakfast.'

The girl looked over and smiled at Frida. She turned around, placing a hand on her towelled head. 'That's what I said. I said, I'm not paying thirty when I can get it for fifteen, mate.'

Estela noticed a rose tattoo on the girl's shoulder blade. It was in the old-fashioned sailor style.

'I'm telling you now, Den, I'm not paying fucking thirty.'

The girl quickly looked around and cast a guilty look at

Frida. She curled in her lips and raised a hand to them. 'Sorry,' she mouthed.

'She did a bad swear,' whispered Frida.

'I know,' whispered Estela.

She turned back. 'Yeah. An hour or so? Yeah. I'll get the bus. Yeah, I know. I'm not being funny, but' – she lowered her voice to a whisper – '*his meow meow is cut to shit anyway*.' Her voice resumed its normal volume. 'Yeah. See you in a bit. Bye.'

The girl cut the call and walked back into the house, smiling at Frida, whose cheeks were bulging with Weetabix.

Frida swallowed her food. 'Mum?' she said.

'Hmm?'

'What's meow meow?'

'You heard that?'

'Yes. What is it?'

'I don't know. Why don't you ask Trog?'

Frida laughed. 'Because cats can't talk, silly.'

Estela tapped her nose with her finger. 'That's what you think, *nena*.'

'Cristián?'

'Hmm?'

'What is meow meow?'

'*Qué?*'

'Meow meow.'

'It's the sound a cat makes multiplied by two.'

'How very helpful you are.'

'*De nada.*'

They were in bed. He on his back, she draped on top of him, rasping her fingernail against the stubble on his neck. Her eyes scanning for ingrown hairs.

'Seriously, Cristián. What do you think it is? I think it's a drug. It sounded like a drug. The way she said it. *Whisper,*

whisper.' She flicked his cheek. 'Stop ignoring me. Have you met them yet?'

'The man, yes.'

'Not the daughter?'

'The one with the meow meow? No.'

They lay quietly for a moment

'Have you painted today?' he asked, his hand wandering mindlessly to her hip bone.

Estela pulled a face. 'Don't ask me that. I told you to stop asking me that.' She traced a swirling pattern in his collarbone with her finger. 'Maybe I'll try tomorrow.'

'OK. Go to sleep.'

Estela rolled away and closed her eyes. She thought about the strip of bricks that separated her house from next door's. Just a wall. And they were doing all these things. Eating, talking, fucking, shitting, laughing. Just a wall between it all.

Estela spent a lot of time in the garden. She needed fresh air and sunshine like a bat needs the dark. When she wasn't keeping house or trying to paint, she was in the garden, weeding, mowing, trimming. Pottering around. When Frida was home from school she helped.

'You be my apprentice gardener,' Estela said to her one day, and so it became a game. Frida wore her green frog wellies and an over-sized pair of gardening gloves and followed her mother around. Sometimes she got bored of picking up the hydrangeas' clipped detritus or collecting muddy clumps of root and bulb for the compost bin and she would go indoors and play with her dolls.

These times Estela might swap her mug of coffee for a small glass of wine. She smoked and gazed into the sky with heavy-lidded eyes, going over old sexual fantasies or re-imagining past conversations.

And every few seconds she'd glance at the girl's attic window.

Why? She couldn't say. She didn't spend a lot of time thinking about the girl, just odd moments. It certainly wasn't a crush; Estela had once performed cunnilingus on a friend while drunk at a house party and the experience had made her feel physically sick. No, she didn't like girls. Perhaps it was simple curiosity. Perhaps she was drawn to the girl in the same way Frida was drawn to the slugs at the end of the garden. Something to look at.

Although there wasn't much to look at, really. The girl would just stand at her open window and smoke at certain times of the day. On the weekend she'd have a bottle of beer in her hand. Music would drift out and reach Estela, its clarity and volume depending on the strength and direction of the wind.

But summer passed, as did autumn. Soon it was too cold to open windows and sit in gardens. Estela didn't see the girl for months and would have forgotten about her completely if it weren't for the screaming arguments she heard through the wall dividing their houses. Either the girl and the father shouting, the girl peppering her Hindi or Urdu or whatever it was with loud, vicious *fucks* and *fuckings*, or the mother screeching at the girl like some Bollywood witch.

Mostly Estela didn't think about the girl at all.

She stood in the middle of the spare room she used as a studio and turned a slow circle, looking at the twenty-plus canvases hanging on the walls. Old paintings, some oil, some acrylic, some guided by an inspired moment and completed in a few feverish hours, others born of a cold, calculated process closer to design than art. *Dog's Eye in Monochrome, April Nude, Tarragona Street Fight, Hello Cuca.*

Estela hadn't painted a thing in seven months.

It was late January. Snowing. She should feel inspired.

She just needed to *force* herself to paint.

She went to the cabinet in the corner that held her paints and equipment. She got one of Cristián's beers and wedged a slice of lime into the bottle neck. She placed it on the windowsill and looked at the snow settling on the cars outside, falling from the smoky black sky and swirling around under the amber beams of the lampposts.

A simple landscape. Just to start with.

She set up her easel in front of the large window. Mixed up her paints, poured some turps into a beaker, sipped her drink and finally started sketching the wintery scene outside.

Once the sketch was complete, she started to add paint, her face pulled into an involuntary grimace.

She stayed this way for an hour, eyes never leaving the canvas. Finally, she stood back, picked up her drink, and sipped at it while appraising the half-finished painting. She scowled. 'Piece of shit. Fucking piece of sterile bullshit. *Coño!* Fucking…*hijo de puta!*'

She grabbed the canvas and ran to the garden, holding it out in front of her like a filthy dog. She kicked open the back door, ran outside into the snow and threw the painting across the patio, screaming, '*Cabrón, hijo de puta!*' It skidded across the snow, face-down. She went and picked it up. Came back. Propped it up against the house, diagonally, and brought her bare foot down against it with a crack. Its wooden backing snapped clean in two.

She dragged a hand through her long black hair, her face crumpling. 'Fucking shit,' she said, quietly, hoarsely. She pressed the heels of her hands into her eye sockets, flexing her fingers. Took a deep breath. Pulled her hands away.

The girl. She was standing on the other side of the fence with a fat pale man. Both were wearing woollen hats and scarves. The man's fingernails were painted black. Dangling from the girl's slack mouth was a long spliff.

They were staring at her, frozen, eyes huge with bemused surprise.

Estela looked back. Her feet were cold.

She turned and walked back into the house.

Spring arrived and with it came warmth. Estela returned to her gardening; she planted sunflowers and lady slippers and trimmed the roses, she tended to the tomatoes and runner beans in the greenhouse. On the other side of the fence Miz was busy at work on his own garden, re-turfing, digging up and weeding his borders, trimming the huge honeysuckle bush near the conservatory that spilled up and out into the Morenos' garden. She could hear numerous birds singing from his garage (an aviary?) and one day she asked about them. Canaries and lovebirds, he told her, before going on to describe the mating habits of these birds and their various temperaments. Other than that, they had brief, forced conversations about the British weather, the price of council tax, the quality of their soil. Mostly they nodded and smiled at each other.

In April, Cristián bought Frida a trampoline that she never grew tired of.

'What has happened to my apprentice gardener?' Estela would say.

'She is bouncing,' Frida would respond, her hair lifting and falling, lifting and falling.

In May the girl opened her windows once more. She climbed up onto her windowsill and dangled her legs out. She was wearing stripy rainbow socks. She smoked, tapping ash between her feet, and drank cans of cola. She looked unhappy and no music played.

Estela pretended not to notice. She swept her patio and hummed a nameless tune.

Most mornings the sky was a pale, creamy blue, and the sun a perfect yellow ball, high up but hot. Then, just before midday, the clouds came, darkening the air, and they stayed all day. It had been this way for weeks.

'Some summer,' Miz said to Estela one afternoon, glaring up at the clouds.

Estela shrugged. It was no good getting angry with the weather.

In the middle of August came a whole ten days of beautiful sunshine. As if sensing that this might be their only chance to enjoy the sun, the whole street (or at least those not at work) stayed out in their gardens, morning till night. Estela read magazines on her lounger or played with Frida, enjoying the smell of barbecued meat that wafted through the street and sipping at her homemade lemon pressé. All around her she could hear dogs barking – the white piggy-faced one a few doors down, the shih-tzu belonging to the lesbian couple, even the beagle all the way across the road – she could hear them all, their operatic yelps and ruffs floating over fences, borne by the warm breeze. She did not care for dogs. She barely tolerated the cat.

The girl, she noticed, never came down to her garden any more. She stayed in her room, clambering onto her windowsill at regular intervals to smoke. One afternoon she drank out of a wine bottle. What did this girl do? Was she a post-grad student? Unemployed? Did her parents know about the drinking? Clearly the family wasn't Muslim – some evenings she had seen Miz and the Bollywood Witch

31

drinking brandy in the garden. They might even be Christians; recently she had read that a third of India was Christian.

Mostly she wondered why the girl was so sad lately.

Tuesday. The last day of the sunshine, according to the weatherman ('Make the most of it!'). A cold front was coming in and there would be rain by the end of the week. Estella woke up at seven to the sound of Frida eating Coco Pops at the end of the bed. She dressed quickly in shorts and a vest, fed the cat, made omelette for Cristián, kissed him goodbye then took herself outside with a strong coffee and a cigarette.

She would do no housework today. It was the last day of the sunshine.

At twelve she made Frida some pasta.

At one she opened a bottle of Pinot Grigio. Last day of the sunshine. She was going to get drunk. Fuck it. She hardly ever let herself get drunk. They would have takeout for tea. And if Cristián didn't like it, he could go and fuck himself.

The girl came to her window for her breakfast cigarette at two. By ten past she was back with a bottle of wine. She looked down at Estela, a shy smile on her lips, and raised her bottle in the air. Estela raised her glass and smiled back.

Should she invite her down for a drink?

No. Maybe later. When she was drunk.

So she drank. And the girl caught up. They opened their second bottles around the same time. The girl raised her bottle. Estela raised her glass.

How funny! How *dysfunctional*. This is what it really means to be British, she thought. Everybody separate behind their walls and everybody drinking.

Around four the girl went and put on a long compilation

32

of slow, downbeat songs. Estela recognised only one – 'The Needle and the Damage Done' by Neil Young. Cristián had *Harvest* on vinyl; he used to play it in the days he still cared about music. She wondered why the girl was listening to sad music on such a bright, beautiful day.

At half four Estela joined Frida on the trampoline. She jumped up and down, her hands holding her breasts in place, screaming with laughter.

'Higher!' shouted Frida.

'Shut up!' replied her mother.

'Go higher!'

'I'll be sick!'

'Higher!'

Estela grabbed Frida in a bearhug and bounced as high as possible.

'Higher!'

'*Poco monstruo!*' Estela kissed Frida on the forehead and released her.

'You can't jump as high as me,' said Frida.

'No, I can't.' Estela climbed down and stumbled back to the lounger. She lit a cigarette and lay back.

At five Estela decided to do some gardening. She watered the sunflowers, which were navel height by now. She paused to vomit into the flowerbed. It splashed the stalks of the sunflowers and sunk, foaming, into the soil. She wiped her mouth with the back of her hand, glancing around – no one saw – and carried on. She got out the shears from the garage and worked on trimming the giant bush that spilled over from next door. She went back to her lounger, picked up her wine glass, took a sip, looked over at Frida, who was still bouncing. She noticed Trog slinking along the drainage pipe that edged the garage roof. He had something in his jaw, something bright yellow.

The girl was slumped against her window frame. Was she crying? Estela could swear she was. 'The First Time Ever I Saw Your Face' by Roberta Flack played, its soft guitar arpeggio flickering on the breeze.

The girl wiped her eyes with the back of her hand. She grew still.

And the Moon and the stars were the gifts you gave
to the dark and the empty skies, my love...

And the question that Estela would never be able to answer with any certainty:

Did she jump or did she fall?

The sun glinted on her lip piercing like a star to wish on.

And Estela dropped her shears and Frida screamed.

And the girl crashed on to the conservatory roof below, rolled down it clumsily, fell again, arms spinning, legs kicking, and landed in the huge, springy honeysuckle bush that Estela had just that moment been trimming.

Frida stopped screaming and bouncing.

Estela ran over to the fence, eyes wild, and looked down into the bush.

The girl lay on her back among the velvet green leaves and twigs, dazed, her arms and face scratched, one leg bent at an awkward angle. She looked up at her neighbour, her drunken eyes opening and closing like the mouth of a landed fish.

Why Do People Have to Be So Mean?

2010

When she sits on the black leather chair it makes a loud creak. Sometimes if this happens the person will laugh and say, 'It was the chair.' I look at her reflection in the mirror. She has no time for jokes, this one. No time for make-up either. Her large cheeks look like slabs of corned beef and her lips are colourless. I wouldn't have time for jokes if I looked like that, I think, and then I tell myself to shut up. You are *such* a bitch. Such a cliché. Her eyes are fixed on the cut-out picture of Halle Berry that I've stuck to the mirror – that's who she wants to look like.

I tilt her head forward and force a comb through her masses of frizzy red hair. Clearly she doesn't use product, which makes all this futile. I grab some clips from the trolley, snap them onto my belt. She's taken this time to pull a book out of her bag. On the cover is a picture of Sarah Michelle Gellar looking stunning but hard done by with David Boreanaz brooding in the background. One of those Buffy novels that only teenagers and die-hard fans bother to read. I should know; I've got a bookcase full of them. She's got to be in her late twenties, so die-hard fan it is. This one's called *Portal Through Time*. I want to ask her how far she's got. I want to ask her who she'd rather shag – Angel or Spike – and what she thinks about that twat, Dawn.

'You doing anything nice tonight?' I say, by way of easing her in.

35

I catch a glint of white as she rolls her eyes. My scissor hand freezes. She turns around. Chair creaks. Her great big moon-face looms around till it's facing me, dead on. Her eyes, I notice, are gun-grey and almost lovely. 'I'm *trying* to read in case you haven't noticed.' She punctuates this statement by curtly flapping her book in the air then turns back, her eyes re-settling comfortably on the page and her expression serious/thoughtful, as if she's reading fucking Nietzsche.

My hands are shaking but my face is neutral – *Insults, darling? They're naught but gnat bites.*

She turns the page and my heart jumps. I try to focus on her hair. I think about snipping off a massive patch, right on the top so it looks like she's balding. *Ripping* a chunk out. Holding her down and scalping her with a sharp blade, peeling the hair and skin away like loose orange peel.

I need to calm the fuck down. Here's a thought – maybe *I'm* the rude one. She's there reading her book and I start with the small talk. Some people really like the sensation of having their hair cut; the fingers fluttering around the ears and neck, the satisfying *snip snip* of the scissors. It relaxes them, the touch of another. It requires silence.

But I only used small talk as a means to ease her into a more satisfying conversation. It was going to be like this:

'You doing anything nice tonight?'

'Uh, not really.'

'Gunna stay in and watch a bit of Buffy, issit?'

'Yeah, maybe.'

'I live for Buffy, me. Never missed an episode.'

That would've been the springboard from which we'd have launched. But no. She wouldn't have it. And look at her now, absorbing narrative as if nothing's happened like some fucking sociopath.

My hands are shaking so bad now that the scissors are clattering about. Her eyes are still on the page but I can see her brows furrowing. My nervous energy must be *such* an inconvenience to her. What I want to do is tilt the chair forward with a violent jerk so she spills out onto the floor, nose first, and then I want to stomp on her head and kick her in the face again and again until her blood mixes in with all the cut hair the way puke mixes in with sawdust and everyone's screaming—

I need to get away from her for a minute. I need a fag.

'I'll be back in two minutes,' I say, jaw like rock.

She frowns into her book. Cunt.

I go through the back, passing Jenny. She's making coffee, waiting for the kettle to boil. Her finger falls out of her nose the second she sees me. I pretend not to notice and go out the back door to the small gravelled car park in the lane. On one side is a Chinese chip shop and on the other there's a tattoo studio, but both these shops have closed gardens and all you can hear is the buzz of a tattoo gun and the sizzle of fat in a wok drifting faintly over the rubble walls. I light up a fag and inhale, my eyes half-closing. School kids from the local Primary walk past, followed by parents or grandparents. Half the kids are Muslim and you hear some customers bitch about how the school has gone down in recent years, and they don't specifically say that it's because of all the darkies, but you know the pricks are thinking it.

The homeless guy who always drinks in the lane walks past, swigging from a bottle of Drambuie. He's going to see me and try to bum a cigarette. Like he always does. With his false charm and his drunken bonhomie, as if he's not a tragic, lonely alcoholic. I imagine him coming up, eyes twinkling in his grubby face, and before he can say a word, me kicking him in the nuts so he doubles over then grinding my cigarette into the top of his head. 'Here's your cigarette.'

But he just walks on by.

Jak likes to joke that I've got PMT. 'You're fucking lucky I'm not a woman – you'd be dead by now,' I tell him.

'Sez, darling,' he says, 'If you were a woman with actual female hormones, I'd run for the fucking hills.'

I start to think of the things I could've said to the bitch.

'Look, there's no need for that kind of tone, hun.'

'Look, I'm a person with feelings.'

'Look, I'm sorry about the small talk, but you were overly harsh in your response.'

But here's the thing. If only I'd had the nerve to stand up for myself in the first place, I wouldn't be feeling this acidic. I'm a people-pleaser, I hate myself for it, and so maybe I'm projecting my hatred outwards. That woman may be rude but at least she has the integrity to speak her mind. Maybe I'm jealous of her?

Maybe she's having a really bad day.

Maybe *she's* got PMT.

Maybe she's homophobic. Or racist. Or both.

Maybe she's jealous of me. Because that's what all mothers say to their shitty kids, isn't it? They're just jealous of you, darling! Here's this woman – fat, ugly and ginger, probably single, no friends, just stays in every night flicking herself silly to Buffy, and here *I* am, attractive and bubbly with perfect hair and creamy-brown Halle Berry skin, asking her about the evening she will spend alone.

Maybe now she's feeling really guilty about her blunt response, and though her eyes are scanning the words on the page, she's not taking them in, is instead thinking, 'Why am I such a bitch? What's *wrong* with me?'

Maybe maybe maybe.

I've had enough of this shit. I'm having a schizophrenic diatribe like fucking Gollum and what I should be doing is cutting hair. I'm just going to get over it. The woman requested no conversation. Big deal. Let's go and slap a Halle Berry haircut onto her big white stupid turnip head in exchange for thirty-four pounds.

I stub out my fag, breathe deeply and stride back into the salon, slapping Jenny's arse as I pass her by because she's a massive fag hag who loves this sort of thing.

The woman is doubled over her book like a beetle. She looks up as I approach. I won't look at her face – it's probably filled with impatience and this will only set me off again. I pick up the scissors and continue sectioning, snipping, shaping. I concentrate on nothing but the hair. I give her texture, bounce. I make sure the back is straight and that it's all symmetrical.

It's been twenty minutes. She reads. I snip. Almost finished. I get out the hairdryer, put a diffuser on the end. The noise clearly irritates her, I can tell by the knotting up of her badly plucked eyebrows.

All dry now. Just a bit of product, clay I reckon, and then some finishing spray.

How good of me to control myself like that.

'There we go,' I say, holding the handheld mirror to the back of her head.

She finally drags her eyes away from the book and glances up at the mirror.

I pan it from left to right, tilting it expertly.

Clearly she loves it, but she doesn't allow her face to betray this. 'Hm. Yes. It's nice,' she says.

I know she's telling the truth because she's not one to hold back her feelings, this one.

'Hang on a sec,' I say, putting the mirror down. I take a delicate hold of her bangs and pull them down so they're in line with her non-existent jaw line. I look, via the mirror, at both sides. She's scrunching up her nose and furrowing her brow again. Her eyes meet mine, via the mirror. 'If you're going to smoke,' she says, 'you could at least wash your hands afterwards.'

Our eyes are locked. Her almost-lovely grey eyes in a toxic relationship with my nutty brown ones. I feel the blood filling up in my ears like the mercury in a thermometer. I want to end her life. Sorrynotsorry. I imagine taking the scissors from my work belt and driving them into her neck, once, twice, three times, leaving three little holes like on a bowling ball, thick red blood spilling out like jam from a doughnut and her gurgling on it and pawing at her throat, saying, 'I'm sorry, I'm sorry, I'm sooorrry!' and I'm saying, 'Too late!' before thrusting the scissors up her nostril, jamming them into her brain and then twisting the scissors, fucking *twisting* them.

Why do people have to be so mean?

I close my eyes for three seconds. Inhale. Fag breath on the exhale. I'm still loosely holding the ends of her hair. She's still looking at me. Via the mirror. Her big doughball face tilted down slightly, mine brooding in the background, both our hairstyles gorgeous, hers copper, mine ice-blue. There's a look of mean intolerance in her eyes. Fear too. Fear is always the thing brooding in the background, I know that much. She's just like everyone else – terrified and trying desperately to hide it. Obviously hates herself. Can't say I blame her.

I smile sweetly, nod my head at her book. 'At the end, right, Buffy writes an anonymous letter to Angelus, he doesn't go with Darla and therefore the future is not changed, and they win the fight against Darla, and everything turns out *great*! And Halle Berry? Deluded, much. You'd be lucky to pass for Meatloaf. That'll be thirty-four pounds please.'

Oh, her face – it's beautiful.

Apricot Ava

2007

Hatima slammed the phone down. This time Gayle had apparently sprained her wrist doing the housework and would not be able to make her shift today, but truly she was having a hangover, everybody knew she was alcohol-dependent. She picked up Mr Evans' care plan and fanned herself – it was hot in this office even with the fan aimed at her face, and it was messy too because Connie was bloody lazy – look: there were her coffee cups on the desk, three of them half-drunk and left to go sour in the heat, and sometimes Hatima wondered if Connie did this on purpose because she was unhappy with being deputy manager only; very bitter, some of these women were. Oh, but it was so bloody hot! It could not be the weather only, because the British sun was a piss drop compared to what she had grown up with, so possibly it was menopause? 'Go to the GP, Mum,' Deena had said to her yesterday, 'you're driving me fucking mental.' 'You are driving yourself mental, with no help from me,' Hatima had responded, stretching across the dining room table and tapping Deena's beer bottle with her fingernail, 'Always you are drinking, like a man, it's very bad for your liver.' Deena had smiled in that sly way and said, 'Always you are mental, like a mental person, it's very bad for your daughter,' and then Miz had dropped his newspaper and said, 'Stop taking the piss out of your mother,' but Hatima had seen how his eyes were shielding laughter. The door opened and Connie came in, ripping off her plastic apron and balling it up.

She stood directly in front of the fan, blocking all the cool air, claiming it all for herself, and Hatima, noticing the sweat patching her underarms, wondered if possibly she was also having the menopause? 'Gayle called in sick,' Hatima told her, and Connie closed her eyes, turned around, pulled open the collar of her tunic and let the fan's air blow down her top. Her undergarments were too tight and her bottom bulged through her slacks in a way that was very unattractive, Hatima thought, and truly she was fat and past the age of fifty, but young-looking with lovely skin the colour of damp sand, and really it was a shame she wasn't making the best of herself. 'She was at the Butchers Arms last night,' said Connie, her back still turned, 'I saw it on Facebook,' and now she turned around, adding, 'I think we should give her a warning,' and Hatima said, 'What you mean is *I* should give her a warning,' and Connie said, 'Well, you are the manager,' and there was that bitterness again. 'I will talk to her first,' said Hatima, taking her cigarettes out of the desk drawer. 'Also, head office rang earlier, and they are asking that we go to Llandough hospital to assess a woman in the stroke ward for respite.' Hatima plucked a Post-it from her crowded PC screen and handed it to Connie, 'She is having vascular dementia and limited mobility. Please, you will do this for me,' (not a request, she made sure, it must not be a request). 'I can't,' said Connie. 'If Gayle's not here then I've got to do the lunchtime meds.' And Hatima slid past her, swiping her thigh on the desk edge to avoid touching her colleague's body, and said, 'You will find time, Connie, please.' Again, not a request. 'Hat, I almost forgot,' said Connie, following Hatima out of the office. Hatima slowly turned around, one of her shoulders stooped

and Connie tightened her mouth to conceal the laughter trying to come out, because for a second there,

Hatima had the look of Colombo turning around to ask his killer question – *One more thing, Mz Jeffries*. 'Ted's flushed his pad down the toilet and his bathroom's flooded.' She stayed long enough to enjoy Old Sourpuss's miserable reaction then turned swiftly on her heel and headed to the common room. Small pleasures could still be had now and again and it wasn't like she was getting them at home; all Simon seemed to do these days was lie on the couch farting along to *The Sopranos*, Josh was up in Loughborough doing his PhD and Sez was doing his hairdressing and never replied to her texts – weren't gay sons supposed to be Mummy's boys? Well, sod him and sod them all. Bring on home time because she had a New York cheesecake and a lovely fat spliff with her name on and a whole week's worth of Corrie backed up on her TiVo box – 'Con!' It was Michelle, coming out of the common room with her eyes huge and wild like bowls of rice pudding with dollops of black cherry jam in the centre. She gripped Connie's shoulders and said, 'I can't find Apricot Ava anywhere!' and Connie gawped into her face, smelling last night's wine and garlic coming out of her pores and breath, and said, 'Have you looked out the garden?' and Michelle nodded and said, '*Everywhere*, Con, I've looked fucking *everywhere*, and so's Benita and Hasna,' and teeny tiny Benita arrived in the hall, flushed and out of breath, and Michelle, with naughty humour in her Jacuzzi eyes, said, 'Escape from Alcatraz,' in a low, Russian accent, and Connie leaned her back against the cool wall and said, 'Fuck,' just that one word, 'Fuck,' almost breathed out, and Michelle said, 'Hatima's going to shit bricks, Con.' 'Indeed she is,' said Connie, 'and *you're* going to be the one to tell her, because *I* have got to do the meds *as well* as fitting in an assessment at Llandough – you can thank Her Royal bloody Highness for that, Mich, she's out having a fag by the way, good luck.' And off she went, rummaging in her pockets for the med trolley keys

and Michelle stood there in the hall, glancing at Benita, who was taking a chewing gum out of a packet of Orbit and putting it in her lipsticked mouth delicately as if for the pleasure of a watching man. 'I'll go and break the news,' she told Benita, 'so why don't you start bringing them through for lunch?' And Benita nodded and said, 'Good luck,' before offering a chewing gum, which Michelle gratefully accepted, because God knows she'd had a skinful last night and Hatima would already be on the warpath over that bloody idiot, Gayle – what was she doing, posting photos of her and that caveman twat of a husband sat in a beer garden the night before phoning in sick? Michelle had never missed a day of work over a hangover, though it was true she'd never once had a hangover – her mother never had either, and she'd drunk like a fish. She entered the laundry room, stepped over a pile of soiled sheets (health and safety violation right there) and went outside to find Hatima sitting on a large tin dustbin next to a pile-up of old Zimmer frames, smoking a cigarette and gazing mournfully at the tool shed. The handyman, a kind, monosyllabic man called George, had died last month of prostate cancer, though why Hatima should be sad about this was beyond Michelle, since she'd never seen the woman talk to George once, unless it was barking orders. She tucked her chewing gum in the gap between molars and cheek and came right out with it: 'Ava's missing.' Hatima blew out her smoke and said, 'Missing?' and Connie said, 'Yes. We've looked everywhere,' and Hatima said, 'Look again.' Michelle slumped her shoulders and stared at Hatima. 'I'm not being funny, Hat, but I have literally searched every room in this building twice, as well as the garden, and so's Benita and Hasna.' Hatima tilted her head back and moaned, her throat bulging like a loaf of bread, and Michelle said, 'Shall I call the police? And the family?' and Hatima ignored this. 'How did she get out?' she said, climbing down off the bin and smoothing down her dark purple shirt, and Michelle said, 'I don't know, but we had the Boots delivery this morning so maybe the door was left open…?' and Hatima rolled her eyes and said, 'I am *telling* them about this! Always I am telling them it's faulty and must be closed with due diligence, but they are not *listening*, Michelle, and now it brings me all this fucking trouble!' and Michelle offered her boss an understanding smile – she *did* understand, because the owners were tight bastards and Connie was useless and spent most of her time in the office playing Candy Crush, but still, she couldn't help but feel a silky ribbon of schadenfreude because of that time Hatima got promoted to manager and *immediately* informed her that she could no longer bring her dog in on the night shift because of 'health and safety' even though Bilbo was adored by the residents and actually, it could be argued, aided in therapeutic something-or-other, whatever the terminology was, and no, he did not have fleas, thank you, and *fuck* you Hatima. 'Let's not call the police,' Hatima said, fingering her cigarette box thoughtfully. 'We'll go to that pub first.' Michelle nodded; Apricot Ava had gotten out before – she was like the raptors from *Jurassic Park*, always testing the fences, which confused Michelle, because how was it a person's brain could be so scrambled by dementia that they were unable to remember their own name and sometimes forgot how to dress themselves, yet put them in a building with locked doors and they suddenly turned into mastermind escape artists – and the last time, she'd been found in the Butchers Arms, drinking half a pint of stout and chattering nonsensically to a family who were trying to eat their Sunday dinner. Ava's daughters had gone apeshit at Hatima over this, one of them even making fun of her accent, which Michelle had found funny, except on the way out she'd heard the woman mutter the P-word and this, for her, had been a step too far. Michelle followed Hatima back inside, passing through the dining room which was beginning to fill up with the top-floorers, and as she walked she imagined Apricot Ava walking into the road and going under the wheels of a huge people carrier, her brittle old body breaking into pieces and her false teeth flying out a spitty bullet, and while Michelle would not particularly mourn the loss of Apricot Ava, who was a pain in the arse, let's be honest, she would mourn a bloody and *senseless* loss, a screeching, smashing, shattered loss – though, thinking about it, a pitifully *quick* ending and better by far than what was coming. Michelle just hoped that by the time she was that old, euthanasia would be legal, and if it wasn't then she was going to hobble or roll her way to the nearest drug dealer, score a bag of smack, inject the whole fucking lot and die with a smile on her face.

Hatima put the car into neutral, lifted the hand brake and got out of the smoke-filled Peugeot, checking once to see if Michelle was following her and marching inside the pub, which she disliked very much because of its smell of sour lager trapped in the carpet and its dull black-and-white pictures of rugby players of the nineteen fifties. She went past the bar, scanning the tables, and asked Michelle to check the beer garden. She went through to the lounge room, which was where the women were often to be found, and there, sat at a table on her own was Gayle, drinking a glass of white wine, and Hatima felt a tired fury all at once, but as she approached she noticed that Gayle's eye was puffed out and red like a baboon's bottom, with only a fingernail slice of eyeball showing, and Hatima's fury became like fire doused with ice water. Gayle looked up and her wine glass froze in mid-air, and then Michelle was there, saying, 'Hat, she's not out there.' Then, seeing Gayle's battered face, she stared with open-mouthed horror, and said, 'I'm going to fucking kill him!' and Gayle stood up and said, 'No, Mich, don't—' but already Michelle was running out of the lounge and Gayle was following, hobbling on her bad leg, and Hatima did *not* follow, she was not touching this situation with a bloody barge pole, truly it was *not* her business, and so she left the pub and returned to her car, ignoring the two women outside who were talking all at once with loud, emotional voices, and she pulled out of the small gravel car park and got onto the road and considered what her options were now, and unfortunately, there was only one: she must notify the police and the relatives of Ava and accept the consequences. She drove down Gowon Road, stopping at a red light and taking the time to light a cigarette, and across the road she saw an elderly Sikh gentleman pouring a carton of lumpy milk down a drain by the kerbside, and further along there was a young white woman stroking a cat that lay flat on its side on the hot pavement. She remembered the one time, early in her own marriage, when Miz had slapped her cheek for an indiscretion and she had grasped his testicles (they had been naked in the bathroom) and twisted them and said, in her mother tongue, 'Do that again and I'll cut them off, do you hear me?' and his eyes had watered terribly and afterwards he apologised and such a thing had never happened again, and truly, Miz was a good husband and very attentive, but she wondered if this would have been the case if she had not handled his testicles like so, because people

48

would do what they could get away with. Yes. They would do what they could get away with. The traffic light turned to green and she carried on down the long tree-lined road. She'd be needing a photograph of Ava to give to the police, as well as knowledge of what she was wearing, and this might be problematic, since often Ava was going up to her room throughout the day to add on extra layers and sometimes Hatima was hearing from the evening staff that, upon undressing her for bed, they were finding five shirts and three underpanties, and also many biscuits hidden in her bra. Apricot Ava had once been a yoga instructor and even now she could, in a standing position, place her hands on the ground in front of her, and she had been vegetarian when she first came to Hillvale, and had moved with such dignity and wore many beads and jewels, but as her capacity for speech and thought degraded, so did her vanity, and furthermore, she started to eat meat again, forgetful of her past diet, and this Hatima had found very sad, and she couldn't pinpoint why she found this more sad than anything else – more sad, for example, than the lady's dignified flowing walk changing into a sly shuffling, or her gentle speech changing into puzzled silence. Sometimes, doing this job, it felt like there was too much sadness to hold. Deena was speaking always of 'negativity' and 'toxicity' and possibly this was passing Western fashion, a nonsense of luxury, but maybe she had a— Hatima pushed on the brakes, her body jolting forward: there, across the road, was Apricot Ava, sat upon a small wall outside a house, with the unkempt homeless man who often could be seen stumbling around the area drunk. She lifted her hand in apology to the angry driver who had braked behind her, noting with amusement that her cigarette remained between her fingers even after such sudden braking. She parked, got out, crossed the road and approached Ava and the homeless man, who were chatting together happily and sharing a bottle of alcohol, and look – Ava was smoking a cigarette also! And with such grace she was smoking it, with her back perfectly straight and her chin tilted, very much like Audrey Hepburn, and what a shame she was wearing a soiled nightgown placed over what looked like two shirts. 'I didn't know you smoked, Ava,' she said, smiling at the old woman, and the old woman smiled back and said, with her old clarity, 'This gentleman here offered me one and for the life of me I could not resist,' and Hatima glanced at the 'gentleman', who was grinning with drunk watery eyes. Ava clamped her strong hand around Hatima's wrist and said, conspiratorially, 'We've been at the cham' too, though I suppose it's too early,' and the man tilted his bottle (it was cider) and said, 'Never too early!' and they both laughed, and Hatima said, 'So what have you been doing, Ava?' and Ava said, 'We've been to see the peacock,' and Hatima said, 'The peacock?' and Ava said, 'Yes,' and the man said, 'And what a splendid peacock it was,' affecting the voice and accent of a refined Englishman, and Hatima couldn't help it; she laughed, almost choking on her smoke, because here she was presented with a demented old woman and a crazy drunk who were imagining peacocks, and truly, what was the difference between the two? The man said, 'She's been telling me jokes,' and Hatima said, 'The one about the apricot?' and the man nodded, smiling, because he had not heard this joke a hundred times coming out of the mouth of a difficult old woman who continuously pissed on the stairlift, and she said, 'I think I need to get her home for lunch, but thank you very much for keeping her company,' and he said, 'It's been a pleasure,' and Ava said, 'It *has* been a pleasure, but the lady is right – I need to get home to my mother, she'll be expecting me,' and the man said, 'Fair enough, wouldn't want to worry her.' Hatima held Ava's hand and led her across the road to her car, looking back at the gentleman, who would probably be moved on soon, told to go somewhere else, sit somewhere else, he was not wanted here. 'Ava, dear,' she said, 'do you know any good jokes?'

Dogs Only

2007

He opened the warm can, anticipating the tinny scrape – a sort of *crrrch* – followed by the *tsssss* of gas hissing out. This was the noise he liked to wake up to. It meant more than singing birds or a boiling kettle. He drained a third then grabbed the sleeping dog against his hip and belched loudly into her ear. Tail started wagging between duvet and mattress, a muffled *thud thud thud*. 'Morning, dickhead,' he said, kissing her between the eyes.

The light shining through the slit in the curtains was the sharp platinum of a bright winter's day. He turned his back to it.

He stumbled to the bathroom, clearing his throat and scratching his armpit. Had a piss, resting one hand against the mould-mottled wall to keep himself steady, splashed the rim anyway. The warm smell of corned beef floated up from the bowl (his urine was starting to scare him). He imagined his liver as a tandoori chicken breast, all lumpy, red skin – he knew what cirrhosis looked like.

He shook off and wiped his fingers on the faded Joy Division t-shirt he'd been wearing for two weeks now. Walked by the mirror. Did not stop to look.

'Cocktail hour,' he said, slapping his hands together and looking at the English Bull Terrier in his bed. *Thud thud thud.* 'Go and have a piss, Pattie.' *Thud thud thud.* 'Go on. Go wee wees. Wee wees? Go on.' The dog stayed. He flapped a hand at her. 'OK, whatever.'

Inside the fridge were fourteen cans of Special Brew, eleven Orangeboom, a tub of Flora Light and half a tomato grown pink and spongy with time. He stared at the tomato, his black-spiked jaw going slack. How long ago did he buy that? Weeks, months? He wasn't sure. Must have been ages – wait. Wasn't him who bought it. It was *her*. To put in a bagel with hummus or some other shit. It *was* months ago. Two to be exact. He grabbed a can and closed the door.

By his third he was ready to open the curtains. A soft white light spread through the bedsit, illuminating every drab surface, every screwed-up chip shop paper. The thirty-plus empty cans lined up along the bottom of the bed glinted harshly. He closed the curtain.

'Bit of music, I reckon. Wha' ju fancy, Pats?' The dog squirmed out from under the duvet, stretched, yawned and approached him, wagging lazily.

'How about some Buckley, eh? Which one, dad or son?'

She circled his legs, still wagging,

'Oh, I see. Not good enough, eh? Well, what would you like?' He cupped an ear. 'What? Bucks Fizz? You tasteless twat.' He got down on his knees and scratched behind her ear. Her white muzzle was still stained by the curly handlebar moustache he'd drawn on days ago. Must've been permanent marker. He had no recollection. 'I'm a bad dad, innit?' he said, smiling sadly. 'Go on, go for a piss.' He led her through to the kitchen and pointed her in the direction of the dog flap. She meandered toward it and jumped through. He stayed on his knees, watching the flap swing back and forth, his head tilted to one side, the smile still there.

Sometimes he enjoyed *Loose Women*, especially when they started getting bawdy or when Carol McGiffin talked about sex. Right now, though, that Coleen fucking Nolan was 'speaking as a mother'. She could stick her kids up her arse. Pattie was lying at the other end of the sofa, by his feet. He stroked her head with his big toe. Dogs all the way.

He scratched his arse, sniffed his fingers. Something he could do now without judgement. 'Swings and roundabouts, eh?' he said to Pattie. What to do with the day? TV wouldn't get good until the evening and he'd cancelled his internet. Two months ago, to be exact.

He grabbed the phone from the table, dialled a number.

A man answered after four rings. 'Hello?'

'Heeeyy, Andrew. What's going on, babes?'

'Oh. It's you.'

'Yeah, it's fucking me.'

'Don't tell me – you want to borrow some money.'

'Oh, the cynicism of you, Andrew! I won't deny that I'm *this* close to getting my utilities switched off and possible eviction, and frankly, I'm astounded that I'm even able to make this phone call. I won't deny that, Andrew, but it's not why I'm calling. For shame, Andrew.'

'You're pissed, aren't you?'

'Well, just—'

'I'm not talking to you pissed, I've told you before.'

'Don't be like that.'

'I *will* be like that. Call me when you're sober and I'll be happy to talk. All right?'

'Fine. All right. How are you doing, Andrew?'

'I *said*—'

'Just tell me how you *are*, Andrew, for fucksake. You're my brother. I haven't seen you in bloody yonks.'

A sigh. 'I've been promoted. I don't expect you to be happy for me.'

'Well, you know the song: "We hate it when our friends are successful."'

'Cheers.'

'I was joking, Andrew. I'm made up for you. How's Meg?'

Another sigh. 'Fine. Going through the menopause.'

'Sounds like fun. What about the evil stepdaughter?'

'She's doing her PhD and I hardly ever see her. Look, I'm going now. Call me when you're sober. Bye.'

'Wait a sec—'

The connection broke. He let the phone fall into his lap. Fucking family. Fuck 'em. Dogs only.

Seventh can. Black and white British film set in a boarding school. Someone was stirring up trouble. Someone else was having none of it. He drifted in and out of the story. Mostly got lost in his own head. Memories, fantasies, tangents. *Her.* Sucking him off in the changing rooms of Topshop; kicking Pattie for pissing in the kitchen; stroking his face and whispering lovethings while she thought he was asleep; telling her friends that he'd hit her when he hadn't. A shove, it'd been.

He shouldn't think about her now. Not on the seventh.

He became aware of Pattie's high-pitched whine. She was on the floor, pacing, moaning. She noticed him looking at her and started wagging.

'What ju want, Pats?'

She gazed at him pathetically, her piggy eyes fixed on his, before walking around in a circle and letting out an obstinate yelp.

'What? It's not dinner time yet. What the fuck ju want?'

More whining. More pacing.

She wanted a walk. Dogs want walks. Fuck. When was the last time he took her out of the house? Three days ago? And that was just a ten-minute job.

'Sorry, Pats. Come 'ere.'

She didn't move.

'C'mon. I'm sorry. I'm too pissed. Daddy's too pissed.'

Another yelp.

He put his head in his hands and felt his eyes burn. His hands closed into fists and he brought them to his temples with a thump. Pattie sat watching him, her head tilted to the side with an alien curiosity. He wiped his eyes with the heels of his hand and sat up straight. There – better. A good cry, that's what he'd needed. What all men apparently needed.

He stretched toward the floor with a grunt and picked up his socks and Pattie got excited. She knew. She always knew. He pulled the second sock straight and recoiled – smeared on the bobbled black fabric was a generous helping of dried jizz peppered with dog hairs and crumbs. He sighed. He could do without socks.

He finished Can Number Seven and threw it over his shoulder. 'Right. Let's go for a motherfucking stroll, shall we?'

It was six o'clock and the weak yellow sun was starting to set, striping the sky the colour of lemon cream pie. He zipped his coat up to his chin and walked fast. Pattie walked faster, puffing away like a small steam train. Normally he'd yank her back, tell her 'No!' in a thunderous man-shout, but today he just didn't have the heart. He was on Gowon Road, a long, straight, tree-lined road that went on for half an hour. It was a boring walk, but quiet – cars went by at a rate of roughly one every thirty seconds.

He'd been stumbling after the dog for fifteen minutes when he noticed the small Alsatian across the road. It was sniffing around its front garden, nose in a clump of grass. The owner, a woman, was coming out of the house dangling a leash. The dog snapped its head up. Noticed Pattie. Its body stiffened, just for a second, and then it was running toward her, large eyes wild with the desire to play or fight or fuck.

His first reaction: 'Ugh.' That's all he had time for. The Alsatian was bounding across the road, the owner calling after it in a panicked yell. And then: thump – a sickening *meaty* thump and a hollow boom like a fist hitting a baking tray as a big silver car smacked into its hindquarters.

He saw nothing – his eyes were scrunched closed. 'Please please please,' he was muttering to himself. 'Pleaseplease pleaseplease.'

He opened his eyes. The dog was scrambling around on the opposite pavement. Adrenaline? Or, like a chicken with its head sliced off, was it running on nerves? The owner was sprinting toward it. The car driver had pulled over to the kerb and stepped out. And Pattie had finally noticed. She tugged on the leash to get a closer look, snorting like a bull, a triangle of fur near her tail spiked up.

The owner caught up with the dog and tried to lift it into her arms. Too heavy. The driver, a gaunt, middle-aged man in thick spectacles, stood watching dumbly from beside his silver Audi. The woman tried again. Still too heavy.

Here was his cue. He ran to the car driver and handed him Pattie's lead. 'Please. Hold her for me.' The man nodded with eyes hugely magnified, not even looking down at Pattie. His face was pale, the T-zone beaded with sweat.

He ran to the woman. 'Can I help?'

'I don't know. I don't know.' Her eyes were pink and wet.

'I'll take that as a yes.' The dog was furiously licking its paw. He picked it up gently, holding it in his arms like it was a baby. 'Where ju want him?'

She pointed to her house.

'OK.' He turned to the driver, shouting, 'Stay there – I'll be back in a minute,' then carried the dog to the woman's house, swaying slightly. The woman ran ahead, opening the door and together they walked into a small hallway.

He inspected the dog in his arms. Its eyes were wild. But no blood or guts or crooked limbs. 'He looks all right, you know.'

'Really? But the car – I – I –'

'Come on, let's put him down. Sorry – bad choice of words. It is a him?'

She nodded her head a little longer than was necessary. The dog went down. Immediately he stood up and walked a few steps, back leg limping slightly. He went up and down the hallway, panting, eyes like diamonds.

'Yeah, look, he's OK.'

She gripped his forearm and gaped up into his face desperately. 'Really? How do you know?' Her face was inches from his. He could smell sweet booze on her breath. Interesting.

'He's walking, isn't he? Leg looks OK. He wouldn't walk if it was broken.'

'Yes, but…look at him.'

'He's probably in shock. Can't say I blame him.' He gently peeled her hand from his arm. 'And I think you might be in shock too, love.'

'Yes. Probably.' She got down on her knees. 'Bilbo! Come here, mate.'

The dog approached her, his big tongue quivering. She took his face in her hands. 'Poor boy. Poor Bilbo.' She touched her nose to his. Tears came, shoulders shuddering. Bilbo shook his head free of her hands and commenced walking, agitated, from place to place.

'Hey, come on. It's all right. He's all right.' He stooped down, placing an awkward hand on her back. 'Look. You're just in shock. You need a drink.'

She managed a nod between sobs. He got up and followed the hall down to a living room. Small, scruffy, but not vile like his own place, not smelly. That was women for you. There was a chunky black TV on a stand, an old, scuffed three-seater with a hideous orange floral design, a lilac carer or nurse's tunic hanging on a radiator, a bookcase filled with DVDs and cookery books, a black coffee table covered in mugs, ashtrays and three empty wine bottles. Ellis Creek Shiraz. Three for a tenner down the local offy. He'd had some himself once. Tasted like blood and vinegar.

He moved onto the kitchen. Again, scruffy but not putrid. The surfaces were clean. Just a few purple-rimmed mugs. An almost full recycling bag was slumped in the corner, by the gas stove. He had a look inside: wine bottles, loads of them. He looked in her fridge: six cans of Grolsch, a hunk of cheddar wrapped in cling film except for one cracked, orange corner, a jar of cranberry sauce, half a cucumber (wrinkled), a tub of Flora Light. And half a tomato. A smile lifted up one side of his mouth.

He found a bottle of wine in her cupboard, grabbed two mugs, one plain blue, one white with 'Wake up to milk' printed across it in yellow balloon writing. He filled them up and returned to the hall. She was still on her knees, rocking now. Bilbo was licking his back paw, slowly, almost lovingly.

'Here, have this,' he said, passing her the blue mug.

'Thanks.'

He opened the front door. There was the driver, still holding Pattie. 'Oi!' he shouted, and both the man and Pattie looked. 'The dog's fine! I'll be out in a minute!' The man closed his eyes and breathed out with relief. No one likes a dead dog. He closed the door, got down on his knees and watched the woman drink the contents of the mug in three big swallows. He took in her face. Dark brown eyes, the iris small, the white huge. Really nice, even with the red rims and gooey eye make-up. Small, thin nose, a large mouth. Mid-thirties maybe. Her hair was walnut brown and neck-length – a bob, isn't that what they called it? He looked at her left hand. No ring.

She put the mug on the floor. 'I should ring the vet, have him checked out.'

'Yeah. Yeah. I would.'

She let out a quavering breath. Looked at the ground. 'I don't usually cry so easily. It's just he's all I have.' She laughed abruptly, flicked her head up. 'I know – tragic.'

He reached out and squeezed her arm gently. Let his hand linger. 'I understand.'

She looked him in the eye. 'Do you?'

'Oh, unequivocally. I was walking the English Bull.'

'That was you?'

He nodded. 'I couldn't do without my Pattie.'

'Pattie?'

'That's my – that's what she's called.'

'Pattie. OK.'

They were sitting close, knees touching. He smiled. She smiled. He drank some wine. Blood and vinegar.

'So where is your dog now? Sorry – all these questions. I'm finding it hard to take anything in.'

'She's outside with the guy who was driving the, um, the car.'

'Oh. I expect he'll be wanting to, er…'

'Yeah. Yeah, I expect so.'

Silence. He cleared his throat. They locked eyes. He felt

his stomach go cold, as if it was filled with ice cream. Her eyes were amazing. Really quite…amazing. She wasn't looking away. Were they – were they having a moment? Did she want him to…yes. Yes. He leaned forward, moved his face up to hers, closed his eyes and pressed his lips against hers.

He felt the air move in front of his face. She was leaning back, horrified.

'What are you *doing*?'

He stood up fast. 'Oh shit. Oh. I'm sorry.' He looked at the floor, running a shaky hand through his greasy hair. 'Really, that was, that was – I'm sorry.'

Bilbo froze mid-lick and watched the two people.

'What the fuck did you think you were doing? Christ.'

He took a deep breath. Looked at her knee for a moment. Tossed back the foul, sour wine and grimaced. 'Shit. I um – misjudged the, uh, the… Sorry. I can't believe I just – sorry. Bye.' He went out the front door and lurched up the garden path. He reached the pavement, took Pattie's leash from the pale, confused man and turned left, the 'Wake up to milk' mug dangling from his finger.

Japanese Flag

1996

The first time I ever had an orgasm it was with my stepfather's electric toothbrush. I remember lying on my bed with the sunlight coming through the window, a fuzzy yellow square warming one thigh. The usual frustration giving way to pleasure, then too-much pleasure.

I put the toothbrush back on the shelf above the sink. I did not wash it.

Mum kicked Dad out when I was fourteen. She said he was a useless, *useless* man and she'd wasted enough time on him already. She'd recently started evening classes doing aromatherapy and she'd made friends with women who wore ethical clothing. They took her along to their Primal Urges dance group where she stomped and panted to African drums. When her divorce papers came through they celebrated with a ritual on the beach, dancing around a campfire with their tits out. She was a new woman. A shamanic divorcee. Dad was still pathetic.

Mum met Andrew at a *Rocky Horror Picture Show* play in the New Theatre. He was Eddie: blue jeans, motorcycle boots, waistcoat. Mum was Columbia: gold-sequinned tux, gold-painted top hat, hotpants. She came home with fake blood smeared down her cheeks and a secret sort of knowledge in her eyes.

Andrew came for Sunday dinner. Me and Mum were vegan but she bought him half a pre-cooked chicken from the Deli at Tesco. He gulped down his meal, skin and all, smiling indulgently at Mum's tofurkey.

Andrew was twenty-seven and worked in computer programming. He was stocky with shoulders like humpback bridges. He wore a faded The Cure t-shirt and green Dr Marten shoes. To be honest, he was ugly. He looked like a gargoyle with pretty eyelashes.

After dinner Andrew drank beers while Mum fluttered around like a dumb butterfly. How was school? he asked me. Was I popular? Did I have a boyfriend? What did I like to watch on TV? What kind of music was I into? I answered obediently. Shit. No. No. *Buffy the Vampire Slayer*. Death metal.

'I used to be a bit of a head banger myself,' he said. 'My first gig was Megadeth.' He looked at me expectantly.

'Who are Megadeth?' I asked.

He frowned. 'Only the best metal band of the eighties.'

I shrugged. I knew who Megadeth were. I just wanted Andrew to feel obsolete.

One night he came to the house with a bottle of 'Seth' African wine. He stopped in the hall, sniffing the air like a hound. 'I can smell blood,' he said. 'Someone's on their monthlies!'

Mum clapped her hands. 'Andrew has an *amazing* sense of smell!'

I put down my homework and went to the bathroom to change my sanitary towel and scrub myself with Mum's face flannel. I felt violated. What kind of dick is my mother dating? I thought, squeezing the brown-red water from the flannel until my hands burned.

*

63

He moved in and immediately redecorated, painting over her dark reds and purples. He favoured oatmeal, biscuit-brown, ecru. He swapped her Indian rugs for grey shags, her Frida Kahlo prints with generic sunsets. 'I don't know why I ever bought that thing,' Mum said, frowning at the pregnant African lady figurine she'd loved three months ago. The chair at the head of the dinner table became *his* chair, the armchair closest to the TV, *his* armchair. He even took over the driving from Mum.

He had claimed all the best chairs.

Mum took on her new subservient role with breathless elation, all but fanning him with lotus leaves and feeding him fucking grapes. I didn't like seeing that.

Her veganism was 'a bloody hoot.' 'Try this meat,' he said to her one dinnertime, holding the fork out, 'and tell me it's not better than that bird food.' She took the beef between her teeth, sliding it off the fork. 'Well?' Mum chewed with big doll's eyes. 'It does taste good.' Smiling, Andrew emptied her cashew bake into the bin. 'Of course it does. That's how we know we're supposed to eat it.'

He carved an extra slice. Looked at me. 'What about you? Fancy a real meal for a change?'

I wasn't crazy for cashew bakes, and in fact, didn't much care about the suffering of animals. I'd only gone along with Mum's veganism in the first place because I was fat and wanted to lose weight. But there was such a thing as having *integrity*. 'No, I'm happy with my bird food,' I said, smile made of glass.

Andrew suggested we have a movie night every Sunday. Bowl of popcorn, cans of pop, curtains closed, lights off. A family. We sat together on the couch, Andrew in the middle, his thigh touching mine like a warm log of shit. I'd push myself against the armrest and end up with red marks on my hip.

Afterwards he'd want to talk about the film. 'I didn't *believe* him in this – his accent was all wrong.' 'Did you get the twist? I figured it out within two minutes.' I sat there picking dead rubbery skin off my feet, shrugging occasionally. After *District 9*, Mum sighed and said, 'You could at least thank Andrew for buying the Pringles.'

I looked at her. 'Is he going to thank *us* for letting him live in *our* house?'

Mum's mouth opened and closed. Andrew's face went like pickled cabbage. 'Are you going to let her speak to me like that?'

Smirking, I nibbled a scrap of foot skin.

I came home stoned and hungry. Mum and Andrew were at the kitchen table staring at a half-smoked spliff and two cans of Orangeboom.

'What the fuck are you doing with my things?' I yelled.

'They were in your bedroom,' said Andrew.

'What were you doing in my bedroom?'

'Looking for a CD.'

'You were looking for a CD in my fucking underwear drawer? Fucking snoop.'

He stood up, cheeks pouched with anger. 'You will *not* talk to me like shit! It's no wonder you're being a cow. You're on your period. I can –'

'Shut up about my fucking periods, Andrew!'

Mum looked at me desperately. 'You're fifteen! You're fifteen and you're doing drugs!'

I scowled. 'Yeah, I'm a real junkie. Who are you to talk? Smoking bongs in the living room with those fucking hippies?'

Mum looked down at the table. 'I don't do that anymore –'

'Exactly,' said Andrew. 'Things are going to change

around here.' He sliced his hand through the air like a politician at a podium. 'This is going to *stop*. Your attitude is going to *change*.' He glanced at Mum. 'We're getting married.'

'What?'

Mum lifted her chin with something like defiance. 'Andrew's going to be your stepdad.'

'And you'd better get used to it,' he said. 'Now go to your room.'

They made me wear a lilac bridesmaid dress. In all the wedding pictures I could be seen staring at the ground. Fat, ginger and bitter, with a big swollen whitehead on the end of my nose. Andrew smiling and lifting a flute of champagne like a jolly king at a feast. He wore his green Dr Martens with his tux to show how fucking edgy he was. Mum wore a classic white wedding dress and her auburn hair was curled and covered with white hibiscus. She looked pretty and happy and brainless.

The reception buffet was all meat and cheese. Not one vegan option. I stared down into my lemonade, my stomach grumbling. Andrew came over. He was drunk. He put his glass of champagne down on the table and crouched down to look me in the eye.

'Why can't we be friends? Eh?'

I could hear him breathing loud through his nose.

He sighed, standing up. 'Fine. I've tried and tried and still you— Hey, Joey!' His face spread into a greasy smile and he raised his hands in the air. His brother came over and they hugged like drunken frat boys, almost toppling over. I picked up Andrew's champagne and spat into it. Placed it back down. Without turning his head away from his brother, Andrew reached his hand around, groped for his glass, and picked it up.

To your health, Stepfather.

One day Andrew came home early from work dripping wet and in a foul mood. Mum's Clio was being MOTd so he'd had to walk home in the rain (he wouldn't use buses because of some article he'd read about all the germs and fecal particles found in the seats).

I was lying on the couch. 'Oh poor, poor you,' I simpered from over my homework.

He snatched the book out of my hands and threw it against the wall. 'You will not talk to me like shit! I am your stepfather!' He raked his hand through his hair, his cheeks all pouched up with anger. 'It's no wonder you're being a cow. You're on your period, aren't you? I can smell it. You're a real—'

'Shut up about my fucking periods, Andrew!'

He grabbed my ankles and ripped them off the couch. 'Get your feet off my fucking furniture!'

I stared at him with cool, dead eyes and slowly walked to my room. I sat on the bed and cried, the words 'Fucking hate him, fucking hate him, fucking hate him' repeating in my mind until they lost all sense.

Deadly nightshade, nutmeg, bryony berries, hemlock, aconite root, death cap, cowbane, jimson weed. Too many oysters can cause paralysis. Too much water will flush all the sodium out of your body and make you drop dead. Then there's food poisoning – poorly cooked meat, poultry gone bad. *Salmonella, E-coli.* Ingesting faeces can give you worms.

Household poisons: bleach and ammonia. Oven cleaner. Paraquat. Rat poison. Wood alcohol. Antifreeze. Ingesting any corrosive cleaning product will burn through your mouth, oesophagus, stomach. Your stomach acid will be released into the trunk of the body where it will dissolve your internal organs. In large quantities rat poison can cause massive internal bleeding followed by death; dizziness, bleeding, nausea, vomiting and diarrhoea in smaller quantities. Drinking antifreeze causes depression followed by heart and breathing difficulty, kidney failure, brain damage and possibly death. I liked that one. The way it starts with depression. I sat crouched over my book imagining Andrew getting sad, really sad, and then dying.

But I didn't want to kill him. Just make him sick for a while.

I settled on rat poison.

The kitchen stank of coriander and cumin and garlic and oil. Lamb madras from scratch. Andrew hummed along to 'This Charming Man' by The Smiths. I was at the kitchen table, pretending to do my history homework. He plated up and went to call Mum. I took out the bottle of powder from my hoodie pocket and sprinkled some into Andrew's curry, swirling it around with my finger to make sure it mixed. I wiped my finger on my trousers and ran back to my seat. My heart was beating fast.

Andrew sat down next to me and poured the wine.

'Aren't you having any with us?' said Mum, sitting down opposite me.

I shook my head.

'You could just pick the meat out.'

'The juices will still be there.'

'Andrew, you could've made a little vegetable one on the side for her?'

Andrew snorted. 'Being a vegan is her choice, not mine.'

68

Mum raised her eyebrows and sipped her wine.

I watched Andrew shovel the first forkful of curry into his mouth, my pen frozen in mid-air. He chewed, swallowed. Frowned. 'I think I might've burned the cardamom again.'

'It's lovely, Andrew.'

He shrugged and sipped some more wine. 'It's not bad. Not as nice as that bhuna I made last month though. That was fly.' He side-eyed me. 'Isn't that what the kids are saying these days? "That bhuna was totally fly. This madras, though, is da bomb."'

'Don't try to talk like the yoot, Andrew,' said Mum.

'I was being ironic,' he said.

'More like moronic,' she replied, flashing me a conspiratorial smile. Still trying to make us a family.

Weeks of this – a sprinkle of powder in his garlic-soaked cooking. Pasta, curry, stirfries. Me, waiting with a banging heart at the table for a turned back. He made jokes about my sudden interest in homework. 'We have a scholar in our midst.' Haha.

He started getting nose bleeds. He'd be watching TV and bright red blood would drizzle his chin. Scarlet droplets the size of pennies appeared on the miserable cadet-grey rug. The coffee table became covered with twists of blood-and-snot tipped tissue. 'Must be the eighties catching up with me,' he'd joke. Mum told him to see a Doctor but he waved her worry away. 'I used to have them all the time when I was little, it's nothing.' Bruises appeared on his arms and legs like thunderclouds. He grew sickly pale. Vegan pale.

*

Mum pressed her hand to his forehead.

'It's just man flu,' he said with a weak smile. A film of blood pinking his teeth.

'*I'm* going to make an appointment,' she said, kissing the tip of his nose. 'I will *make* them take it seriously.'

'I'll be fine.'

'You're a sick man.'

'*You're a cunt,*' I whispered.

Mum went off to make the call. It was half-term. I was reading a Poppy Z. Brite book about gay vampires. Mum came back and told Andrew he had an appointment for half four.

'You're a star,' he said.

His eyes were full of love for her. But so what?

Mum went to the shop. Andrew lay on the couch in his crisp white boxers, one arm laying limp, knuckles grazing the carpet. His legs were chunky and hairless. When he shifted onto his side he lifted his leg and I saw his smooth pink bellend in the gap between cloth and thigh. He fell asleep. A wad of baby-blue tissue skewered into one nostril.

This is my stepfather, I thought. This is my stepfather who has lobotomised my mother with his dick. His eyelids quivered. He looked peaceful. Blood drizzled from his free nostril, running down his cheek to the cushion. I felt bad watching that blood flow. I don't know why. Maybe because he was asleep. Powerless. De-throned. His leg twitched. I noticed a small red dot like a bindi on the crotch of his shorts. Blood. I watched as it slowly spread into a poppy, then a rose. A lovely red against his white boxers. A Japanese flag.

'Who's on their period now?' I said.

Go Play with Cucumbers

2007

Watching *Blue Planet*. Neon fish living on the seabed, miles and miles down, carrying their little lanterns like monstrous wartime nurses. Lying on the couch drinking cocoa, listening to Attenborough's reassuring voice. But I'm not reassured. She isn't back. Lou. Said she'd be back by ten. Just 'popping' to her friend's house, Kimmy's. She was 'popping' over to smoke her cigarettes and drink her vodka and listen to her talk about the girlfriend who couldn't take a dildo because she'd been abused as a child, and well, she was understanding, didn't want to push things, but c'mon, it'd been, like, five months, just lube up and shut up. That's Kimmy. Lou lets her get away with this kind of thing because she naively assumes that a woman would never be so horrible, not for real, and also, everything Kimmy says is veiled by sneaky layers of irony so Lou can never tell if she's being a prick. I can.

So. Kimmy: twenty-four, pale and clammy with a face like a skinny triangle, a hooked nose, a small Punch and Judy mouth, thick black eyelashes and one of those hairstyles with half of it shaved off. Predatory and man-like, loves turning straight women. Fancies herself a photographer. Likes to take 'tasteful' pictures of underage goth girls with shaven fannies.

'I don't think Daddy's coming home,' I say to Tulip, my black and white Shih Tzu. Tulip licks my knee then rests his chin on his two front paws. I run my finger round the inside of the mug, licking off the bitty cocoa froth. I have a bad feeling in my belly. I try to concentrate on an octopus with an electric-green filament inside it.

Next morning. Trying to get on with things; showering, washing the dishes, brushing the dog's teeth. Lou's phone is switched off. That bad feeling in my belly, a mushroomy feeling.

Around eleven I'm on the couch, TV on, usual late-morning crap, a vacuous redhead going on about prostate cancer. I should be aware of it. Prostate cancer. Me and everyone else should know that it exists. OK. The front door opens and in comes Lou. The first thing I notice, she isn't wearing a bra under her top. Her tits hang low and her pistachio nipples are pointing at the coffee table. Second thing – all her mascara and eyeliner is messed up and smudged – her eyes look like centipedes squished into the ground by a cruel shoe.

I say, 'What have you done?'

She drops to her knees and starts crying and nuzzling my knees with her face. That mushroom feeling in my belly disappears. I still have a bad feeling, but it isn't mushrooms anymore. It's something icy and sick.

'What have you *done*?'

She looks up at me.

'You slept with her, didn't you?'

Just looks at me.

I push her head away and she rolls back onto her arse. 'For fucksake, Lou! You're a fucking tramp!'

'I don't remember any of it! I blacked out!'

'Oh, well that's OK then!'

'Polly, listen to me, *please*.' Eyes so earnest. 'One minute we were just drinking and then…' She cups her face with

72

both hands. 'I just remember coming back to myself, you know, out of the blackout, and she was on top of me, and I freaked out and pushed her off and smashed up her bedroom.' She rolls up her sleeves. 'And I did this.' A few superficial scratches like red biro that's running out. 'I wanted to kill myself.'

'You should have.'

She grabs my knees again and does that nuzzling thing. 'Please. I'm sorry. Please. Please.' And she carries on saying please in a strained crying-voice and nuzzling my lap like a cat with mange on its face. 'It wasn't me. It wasn't me. You know I wouldn't fuck her sober. She's disgusting.' She pulls a face. 'She's *disgust*ing. I *hate* her.'

I push her onto her arse again. 'Don't tell me what I know.'

Sitting out the back on a white plastic chair, legs sprawled out, Pepsi can on bare thigh. Nice weather – some flat-bottomed cloud here and there but mostly sea-blue sky. I wish the weather was shit. I don't want to be reminded that this could have been a good day. Lounging under a tree at the park listening to reggae on a portable radio. Me and Lou drinking chilled pear cider, her head lying across my stomach.

Deena's dad is trimming his bushes next door. There's the snip-snip of garden scissors and a million birds singing and twittering from his aviary. Deena's attic window is flung open and sometimes I see the swish of her black hair as she moves around inside. Fucking Deena. She's one of those straight women who always flirts with dykes to prop up their own fragile self-esteem. Me and Lou are always joking about one day calling her bluff. Grabbing her head and pushing it down and saying, 'Go on then, eat my pussy if you're so curious.' The garden over I can see the little Spanish girl bouncing on her trampoline. Deena's dad wipes his face, squinting.

I must look terrible. I'm no beauty to begin with, but here I am in a pair of blue gingham boxer shorts, sickly white legs with dark three-day stubble on the calves, a Kenneth Williams T-shirt, the top of his oohing face stretched by my massive tits. Hair fluffy from my shower this morning. New lip piercing all pussy and infected. I look like an ugly dyke. I shouldn't care at a time like this, but there we go.

Lou is inside. Cutting herself probably. She'll come out any minute dripping, Tulip with her. Tulip likes drama. All I can think of is Kimmy's pinched face. I pull a face at the sun and drink my Pepsi. The guy next door, not Deena's dad, the other side – the alky with the English Bull Terrier, he comes out and sits in a dirty red deckchair and opens a can of lager and his dog jumps on his lap and sits looking into the distance with a windswept face both dumb and wise.

I know this is awful, but there's always a tiny part of me, like a lamp in the corner of a very large, very dark room, which lights up when This Kind Of Thing Happens, a part that is happy because I have an excuse to vacate everyday life. The next few days I don't have to bathe or brush my teeth or diet. I get to opt out. It's a small miserable thrill.

Fifth can. Full sugar Lilt. Still out the garden. Mushy thoughts dripping like thick soup down an hourglass, turned back over, same drip, over and over. It all add up to this: I should dump Lou but I don't want to dump Lou. We were going to have kids one day. I really don't want it over.

Tulip wanders in and out, sometimes barking at his arch-nemesis the English Bull, sometimes sniffing my ankles with his small wet nose or lying on the grass, panting, surrounded by dandelions and drying turds. Deena's dad's gone inside but the other neighbour is still there with his can. I hardly know this man. Clearly he has a drink problem.

I heave myself up from the chair and go to the fence, which is rotting and leaning.

I lift my can in greeting. 'Hello.'

He nods and lifts his own can. Dark hair and messy caveman stubble, Liverpool strip, worn jeans. His dog comes over to the fence and I dangle my arm down so it can sniff my hand.

I say, 'So what are you celebrating?'

He does halfway between a smile and smirk. 'Oh, you know. Life. Wonderful life.'

'Amen.'

He says, 'Where's your partner today? I assume she's your partner.'

I say, 'What gave it away?' and he laughs. Because I'm an obvious lesbian. Funny. 'She's inside. Feeling sorry for herself.'

'Well good luck with that.' He drains his can and crushes it. Stands up.

I say, 'Can I just ask you a question?'

He looks at me.

'Has anyone ever cheated on you?'

His eyes do a couple of taken-aback blinks. 'Uuh. Sure. Yeah.' I love provoking this reaction from people. Suddenly veering off from small talk, Getting Real. Lou says that I do it because I want to be admired. 'My last girlfriend actually,' he says. 'Woman who used to live here with me? Do you remember—'

'What did you do? Did you leave her?'

He looks at the floor a while, thinking. Comes over to the fence. Spilled food on his top, something brown, like curry sauce, the type you get in chip shops. Dark eyes. He tosses the crushed can into his weedy, flower-less flower border. 'No, I stayed with her. For a while. I shouldn't have done.'

'She cheated again?'

'No. It's just she wasn't really sorry. She had all these justifications.' He puts his hands in his pockets, takes them out again. 'I wish I'd made her suffer a bit. Earn her forgiveness.' He looks at me. 'I know that sounds horrible.' He looks through me a while, his thoughts in the past. I wonder about his girlfriend. I don't remember her. I do night shifts and sleep most days. Maybe it was her who started up a flower border?

He says, 'Do you watch *The Simpsons*?'

'I used to, when it was good.'

'Did you see the episode where Apu cheats with the Squishy Lady?'

'Probably. I'm not sure.'

'Well Apu is married to Manjula, remember? And he shags the Squishy Lady in the Kwik-E-Mart. And Manjula finds out.' He touches the fence and it gently rattles. 'So she makes up this list of things Apu must do in order to be forgiven. Things like eat a light bulb, change his name to Slime Q. Slimedog. I think he had to get a cartoon published in *The New Yorker* too. So anyway, Apu does these things and Manjula takes him back.'

I say, 'So I should make my girlfriend eat a light bulb?'

He shrugs, laughing. There is something kind in his eyes. Something good and easy. Even while he's talking about vengeance, it's coming out of him like heat from freshly baked bread. For a second I contemplate inviting myself over and having a drink with him, and maybe, at that point when night and drink are mixing like good soup, pulling his dick out of his smelly jeans and sitting on it. Something like that. But I won't do this. Not because I'm incapable of such spite but because I don't like dick enough.

He says, 'Anyway. My two pence' worth. Good luck.' He nods a goodbye and walks away, a little unsteady but not so you'd notice if you weren't looking. His dog follows, wagging its tail, and they go inside. The sun is setting.

On the way to the corner shop I pass an ugly old tramp with a scruffy beard. Swaying, bleary-eyed, carrier bag bulging with cans. He says, 'You look like you need cheering up,' and I say, 'Mind your own business,' and he says, 'Where do baby apes sleep?'

'Don't know. Don't care.'

His smile huge: 'Apricots.'

I say, 'Go and fuck yourself,' and he does a little salute and says, 'Will do.' Which almost gets a smile out of me. I get to the shop, buy some Dr Pepper and a large cucumber wrapped in plastic. The tramp's gone but there's a puddle of piss on the pavement. Salmon-pink sunset reflected in its surface.

Lou has this thing about cucumbers. She hates them. The taste, the texture. If I've eaten a cucumber sandwich or just had a couple of slices in a salad, she refuses to kiss me until I've brushed my teeth or used mouthwash. She has bad associations. Like once, when she was four or five, she watched a small boy in the playground eating a sandwich. He had a snot bubble. It grew as he ate, a mouldy yellow bulb, till it reached the size of a marble and popped and dripped over his chewing lips. It was the cucumber in the sandwich she could smell the strongest. She threw up.

Bad Association Number Two. Lou came out at fourteen. Everyone knew, the whole High School. She even had a girlfriend, a fat Goth who called herself, no word of a lie, Morticia Filth, and they'd hold hands in the street. In the 90s. Pontypridd. Most people left Lou alone because she was weird and angry – she once kicked a boy so hard in his balls he went into shock. So. One day she's on the school bus coming home and there's these bitches from the year above sitting behind her. They're sneaking crisps onto her shoulders and sticking chewing gum in her hair. She's just sat there all still and charged. I can imagine her eyes growing darker and more psycho with every tentative crisp placement. She's electric sometimes, Lou. When she's mad, she has eyes that would give you cancer if they could. Eyes that spit. And Lou, she gets fucking mad. She spins around and shouts, 'What the *fuck* are you doing?' And the main girl, a sixteen-year-old cunt called Maya, gives her the old teeth-sucking, brow-arching, bitch-eyed head-slant and says, 'Why don't you go play with cucumbers, *Lesbo-Lou*?' And my crazy electric Lou throws herself snarling at Maya – I can just see it – and starts pummelling and scratching and screeching, and Maya doesn't have a chance. By the time the other teens on the bus pull her off, Maya's face is pink and clawed and bloody and Lou has a handful of Venezuelan hair in her fist. 'You fucking dyke!' shouts Maya, crying, as Lou runs down the aisle and gets off the bus. Lou watches it drive off and sees everyone at the window either laughing or flicking tongues between vee'd fingers or staring shocked, and she goes down on her fishnet knees and cries, the long black hair still in her fist.

She's sat at the kitchen table, face blotchy from crying. I drop the cucumber in front of her. Pull a chair out and sit on it so we're facing.

'Why don't you go play with cucumbers, Lesbo-Lou?'

She stares at me. I can't see blood anywhere so either she's resisted the urge or they're on her thigh. 'That's fucking callous, Polly.'

I shrug.

'So you want me to fuck myself with a cucumber? Is that meant to be symbolic?'

'I don't want you to fuck it, Lou. I want you to eat it.'

'*Eat* it?'

I nod.

'So what's that going to achieve?'

'It'll make me feel better.'

'I had no idea you were so Old Testament.'

I crack open a Dr Pepper. 'Well, now you know.'

She says, 'I don't know if I could physically manage it,' and she looks down at the table, a fat teardrop falling from her eye and landing near the cucumber. I feel bad. I feel like I shouldn't be doing this, like doing this is heartless and power-playing. But I also feel like I *must* do this. She looks back up at me. 'I'm not sure I can physically keep this down.'

'Well I'm not sure if I can just forgive you and stay with you.'

Another teardrop.

I say, 'Don't you think you should try and earn forgiveness? I'd want to if I was in your place. If that makes me Old Testament, so be it.'

'It makes you kind of sadistic.'

'You're probably right.'

She stubs out her fag and pulls the plastic off the

cucumber, palming it down like a foreskin. She sniffs it, frowns. Gets up, looks in the drawer by the sink and pulls out a flimsy Spar carrier bag. Sits down, puts the bag on her lap. Takes a bite of cucumber. Chews tortoise-slow, grimacing. Swallows.

'Nice?' I say.

Her eyes spit at me. 'Fuck off, Polly.' Another bite. 'Fuck.' She does a long wavery in-breath. Swallows. And another, and another. It's slow going. Tulip comes in and puts his paws on her lap. She smiles at him bravely like it's the last time she'll ever see him. The cucumber is half-gone. She chews, swallows. Retches once, twice, three times. A lady. Brings the Spar bag to her face and vomits. Water and foam and pale green lumps.

'Ugh.' She looks at me with dizzy pathetic eyes. I look back, cool as a...well. She gags again and more pulp falls into the bag. She makes a little crying sound and picks out a chunk the size of a kidney bean. Puts it in her mouth. Face like a bedpan. She opens her eyes and looks at me with misery, so much misery. Hundred per cent wretched. And then suddenly something passes between us, I'm not sure what, and we burst into laughter, hard, deep laughter which fills the room like a panic of brown doves.

The I-Love-You Jar

2010

Day 1

The rice was cool in the pan. Sez sniffed it.

'I just love how rice smells – it's such a clean smell. Ya know?'

He transferred the phone from left to right hand, and rested his back against the fridge door. Jak started yacking on about wholemeal rice versus white rice, which was beside the point.

Sez had read an article on his Facebook feed recently about a Japanese doctor, Masaru Emoto, who conducted a rice experiment whereby he'd put two separate portions of cooked rice in airtight containers, one with a sticker saying 'Thank You' and the other saying 'You Fool', and instructed schoolchildren to say the labels out loud every day upon passing the jars. The Thank You jar, after 30 days, was barely changed, while the other was mouldy and rotten.

'What are you going to call your jars?' Jak said now.

'Well, originally I thought the good one could be Willow and the bad one could be Xander, who as you know, I fucking detest. But then I thought, wouldn't it be more fun if they represented *me*? Since I'm a narcissistic twat and everything is about me, natch.' He laughed. 'So one's gonna be called Baby and the other's gonna be Bastard. Cuz sometimes I'm your "Baby", other times I'm a complete bastard.' He picked up a glass of orange juice from the kitchen table, rolling his eyes at Jak's usual sweet affirmations. 'Thank you, darling, thank you. But I'll show you how much of a bastard I can be when I get you into bed tomorrow. Grrr!'

He said goodbye and turned back to the rice, moving the pan onto the counter. He measured out two piles and spooned them into two identical glass jars. He pushed the stoppers down, making the air gulp, and stuck a sticker saying 'Baby' on one jar. It had love hearts doodled in the corners. He stuck a 'Bastard' sticker on the other jar – devil horns coming out of the B. 'Rice experiment commence!' he said to the empty kitchen, clapping his hands over one shoulder like a Spanish dancer.

'You know what I don't like about you?'

He was sitting on the floor by the wardrobe, holding the jar on his lap. It was dark out. The grey-veined moon, visible through the window, was larger than usual. 'You're selfish. Possibly more so than the average person.'

He pulled a cigarette out of the pack and lit it. 'Hark at you with your Camel Lights. You're so fucking cool and you want everyone to know it.' He tapped ash onto the carpet and rubbed it in with his thumb. His mother had bought this carpet for him. 'You know what else I don't like about you? Your ears. They stick out too much. They make you look retarded. Oh, and there's another thing right there – you use words like retarded. But you're so fucking liberal that you can't *possibly* be bigoted. Yes, you're one of those.'

He put the jar back in the wardrobe, next to his running trainers and a coiled up skipping rope. He pulled out the other jar, smiling.

'Hey, Baby. My gorgeous.' He sat the jar in his lap, one

arm cradling it. 'Don't listen to all that shit. You're a good person. You are. You have a good heart, and that's all that matters.' He blew smoke away, over his shoulder. 'You know what else? You're handsome. Look at your eyes.' He fluttered his lashes. 'Such an unusual colour. Your eyebrows are perfect – plucked *just* enough but not so much that they look faggy.'

'Anyway. Bedtime.' He kissed the jar, his lips squidging the glass like a tentacle sucker.

Day 2

He got in just before midnight. He sat on his bed, took out his phone, tapped out a text, slid to the floor, and crawled on his hands and knees to the wardrobe.

'*Bonsoir*, ricelets. Apparently, I'm not supposed to be handling you.' Tonight, a drag queen had lectured him about ways in which Dr Emoto's experiment had probably been a con. 'Best get some space between you.' He moved the jars apart, arranging them at opposite corners of the wardrobe. 'See, if I touch you then my hands could generate heat and that might affect the outcome. According to the most minging queen in drag herstory.' He lay on his stomach. 'And obviously I'm going to want to touch you, Baby, a lot more than Bastard over there, because Bastard is a disgusting bottom and he's probably riddled with STIs.' The laugh turned into a smoky cough.

'So. Which one first?' He pointed his finger at one jar, then the other. 'Hmm. You.' He shuffled over to the left side and glared at Bastard. 'Better get you over and done with. Like a prostate exam. So. Where were we? Oh, yeah. Handsome. Ha. Look at all those blackheads in your nose. Look how crooked your bottom teeth are. You *think* you're

83

beautiful, but you are sadly deluded, I'm afraid. And how small is your dick? Hmm?'

He smoked, his almost-green eyes on the sticker, his face in shadow. 'You know, Mum was right. You're toxic. And tonight, Jak was saying all these nice things. "Oh, you're so *open* about everything, you're so honest; I know where I am with you." Bollocks. Your so-called refreshing honesty is a ruse. It *seems* like you're being honest because you say shocking things that apparently no one else would say, but underneath there is so much bullshit and crap. And one of these days Jak's going to find out the truth and he's going to dump you. You know that, don't you, you fucking alcoholic?'

His cigarette ash was almost an inch long and about to collapse. He tapped it into his palm. 'Right. I've had enough of you.' He shuffled over to the other jar. 'Baby? I'm just going to say one thing: five inches. I'll say it again: five inches.' He cupped his hand behind his ear. '"What's that?" you say. I'll tell you. It's the national average. When erect. And what is yours? You know what it is, you silly old thing! It's five point three. I'll say it again. Five point three.' He leaned in closer, touching a spot on the carpet like it was Baby's hand. 'Jak certainly has no complaints, am I right?'

He stubbed out his cigarette on the wardrobe, coughing. 'And while we're on the subject of drink,' he said, 'how about we debunk that motherfucker already? Alcoholic? As if! You drink something like, what, twice a week? Get over yourself. Basically, you're fine. You are the queen of self-awareness and your hair is fucking fierce.' He blew the jar a kiss. '*Nos da*, beautiful one.'

He shut the wardrobe door, hesitated, then opened it again.

'I can't believe I just missed the opportunity.' He moved

Baby over an inch and pointed at Bastard. 'No one puts Baby in the corner.'

And laughing hard, he stood up, took all his clothes off, got his lube out of the bedside drawer and sat at his PC.

Day 5

The bedroom door slammed open and bounced back shut.

'Shit.' A muffled voice.

The door kicked opened again. Sez stood there, head lolling, eyes closed.

'Come on, Sez, walk with me,' said Jak, tall, triangle-shouldered, short blond hair, one muscled arm covered in grey-tone tattoos.

They squeezed through the door together, hips scraping the frame. Jak half-dragged, half-led him to the bed and dropped him on the mattress.

'Next time you suggest shots I'm saying no,' said Jak. 'Now let's get you undressed.' He unzipped Sez's fly and started tugging at the waistband.

'While you're down there.'

Jak rolled his eyes. 'So you're alive then?'

'Hmmm.'

'I'll take that as a yes.' He gradually undressed him down to his boxers. 'Sez. Baby. I think you should go to the toilet before you pass out. Sez?'

'What?'

'I said I think you should use the toilet. Sez?'

Sez flapped his hand. 'I'll be fine.'

Jak went to the door. 'I'll get you some water.'

'Jak?'

He turned around. 'What?'

'Love you.'

85

Jak smiled. 'I love you too, you bloody idiot.'

Sez rolled onto his stomach and groaned. The turquoise wings tattooed onto his shoulder blades rippled. He lifted his head up and looked around the room with bleary eyes. 'Jak? Jak?' He groaned again and dropped his head back onto the pillow, closing his eyes.

Jak came back in holding a pint of water. 'Sez,' he whispered. 'Sez?' He stroked Sez's back. 'OK, sleep it off.' He undressed, laying each article neatly on top of a chest of drawers. He was wearing white briefs and he had a Japanese design tattooed on his back – pink lotus, grey scaly fish. He went to the PC and checked his emails. Noticed an open writing pad on the desk, next to a plate covered in toast crumbs. In bubbly writing at the top of the page: 'Sezzer Jeffries' Super Clinical Professional Grown-up Scientific Experiment!' Followed by 'Day 1' and some scribbled observations. The latest observation read, 'Day 4 – No change.'

Jak smiled. He went to the wardrobe and opened it, getting down on his knees. 'Well, hello there. Sez has told me all about you.' He peered at the jar on the left, eyes squinted. 'Bastard. I hear you're a real nasty character. And Baby. Good evening. I think I'd like to start with you.' He sat on his bum and crossed his legs.

'I'll be honest – I think you're wonderful.' He spoke in a low voice but it filled the silent room. 'When we first met – remember you were cutting my hair? When you were still working at Toni and Guy? Every time your hand touched my ear I felt this electricity. It was lush.' He grinned to himself. 'You're just…lush. I feel very lucky.' He smiled into his lap like a strange and happy child, hands placed neatly on his hairless thighs.

He turned to Bastard. 'I guess it's your turn. I'm not sure

what to say to you. I guess you drink too much. But then, you can go weeks without drinking, so…I don't know about that. Um. I guess your –' he glanced at the bed and lowered his voice to a whisper 'I guess your dick isn't very big. But then I'm no size queen.' He lifted a finger at the jar. 'In fact, I once had to go to A&E with lock-jaw after blowing this one guy. Literally the most embarrassing thing *ever*.' He shook his head. 'I'm not very good at being mean to you, am I?'

He got up and quietly closed the wardrobe doors.

Day 6

His blue hair lay flat and greasy on his head. A cigarette dangled from the corner of his chapped lips. 'I feel rough, ricelets, really rough.' He bent over coughing and brought up tar and phlegm. He swallowed, pulling a face. 'Minging.' He stubbed out the cigarette and picked up a glass of fizzy orange Berocca.

'Right.' He turned to Baby. '*Bore da, Baban*. Or *prynhawn da* as the case may be. You know, you were great last night. Really on fire. Every joke landing. Sometimes you just need a blow-out, don't you? You work all week, you work *hard* putting your hands in people's shitty hair and listening to them talk about their boring lives, so yeah, you get to Friday night and you have a few Sambucas, sorrynotsorry.'

He got onto his belly, elbows and forearms on the carpet. 'You know, Baby, you shouldn't be so down on yourself about your ego. You can't go through your whole life hating yourself. Fucking burning yourself with fag-ends like a teenage girl and – and letting gross nasty men fuck you. You have to live with yourself until the day you die, so you might as well work on being *into* yourself. Or at least thinking you are. I don't know. One can never be sure.' He took a sip of his drink, wiping his lips with a finger. 'And you know your faults, don't you? As this experiment is in fact proving.'

His head flipped to Bastard. 'Yeah, and you think you're so fucking wonderful for knowing those faults. "Oh, I'm so self-aware!" As if it redeems you. As if just acknowledging something makes it OK. Even now you're silently congratulating yourself on admitting this, aren't you?' He shook his head like a disappointed parent. 'You're so self-obsessed you even had to make this experiment about *you*!'

That was quite funny actually. He smiled, grinding his cigarette into the ashtray and shuffling forward a little. You had to laugh. 'And let's address this drinking, shall we? Just a little blowout? Don't insult your own intelligence, you stupid fag. You *know* the nature of addiction. It's not about how *often* you drink. Just admit it. You have a problem. You have blackouts. And that thing you did last night with – I can't even say it.' He wrapped a hand round his eyes. 'You can't even say it. You're just going to keep talking, keep talking, la la la, like it never happened, oh *yes*, you're *sooo* fucking self-aware, hurrah hurrah, well done with that, yeah, so self-aware that you're going to block it out and spend the day distracting yourself by watching guys eat their own cum on chat roulette and bingeing season five of fucking *Buffy*, which is a TV show aimed at teenage girls by the way, you fucking loser, and every time Jak texts you're going to feel this little slither of self-hatred, and so you should.'

He slammed the door shut. The rice quivered.

Day 9

Curtains closed. Fuzzy warmth oozing out of the slit down the middle, otherwise, darkness. He was sat on the bed, legs crossed. Manga Y-fronts, white T-shirt, pink woollen slipper socks. Both jars of rice on his bedside table, separated by a bottle of vodka and a carton of orange juice. His cigarette cherry slowly moved in the gloom. It was noon. He'd never felt so shitty.

He picked up his phone and dialled a number. Straight to answer machine again.

'Jak. Please. Just answer. I just wanna – I don't know…please just answer. Jak. Jaaaak.' He breathed a long sigh out of his nose. 'OK. Fair enough.' He dropped the phone back on the duvet, took a long swig of his drink, and picked up Bastard.

'You knew this would happen, didn't you? You *so* knew.' He tilted his chin and burped airily. 'You're a cheating bastard, Bastard.'

Clamping Bastard between his thighs, he reached over and picked up Baby.

'You really love him. You do.' He smiled, eyes sad. 'Remember when he quit smoking and he saved all that money? He'd been putting all the fag money into a jar. A bit like you, only bigger. And not so pretty.' He smiled, the tip of his tongue poking through the gap between his top and bottom teeth. 'He wanted to spend the money on a new tattoo, didn't he? And one day he had enough, and you both took the jar to the bank and swapped it for twenties. And by the time you came home, he'd lost it, the fucking numpty.' He shook his head, still smiling. 'So you both re-traced your steps and even looked in that bin where he'd dropped his sandwich wrapper. But you couldn't find it. You took him home and he sat on the bed and he looked so sad it broke your heart.' He placed a hand on his breast. 'He didn't have a lot of money and he'd been so proud of himself for quitting. So you went back outside pretending to have another search, but instead you went to the cash point and took the money out of your own account. Even though you couldn't afford it. And he was so happy when you came home. "You bloody dickhead, you left it at the bank!"'

He smiled a broad and gloomy smile, eyes glistening in the dark like glasses of milk. 'And you never told him the truth and he still doesn't know. And you decided that it wasn't a selfless thing to do because it gave you too much satisfaction, it made you feel *good* about yourself. But it was a nice thing to do. And nothing can take that away.'

He sipped his drink thoughtfully. 'Or maybe I'm wrong about that.'

He placed Baby back on the bedside table and nudged it away from himself with the tips of his fingers.

He brought Bastard close to his face, his nose touching the warm glass. 'You know what, Bastard? The worst thing about this is you'll never learn. And you'll never stop. And you don't even know if it's the drink or just your nature.'

He stared at the wall, a tear fattening on the precipice of his lashes. 'You didn't even *fancy* him. What the fuck is wrong with you?' He blinked slowly, head swaying a little. 'Why don't you tell Baby how it isn't your fault? Go on. Tell Baby about your bad upbringing. Like that accounts for everything. Your mother was a nasty cow and you've been damaged and it's not your fault. Boo fucking hoo.' He wiped his eyes and stared at the jar with bleary resentment. 'It *is* my fault. It's always been my fault.'

He stuck out his leg and kicked Baby onto the floor. The jar landed hard against the carpet and bounced, rolled, settled, the still-clean rice spreading out like a dune.

It's a Beautiful Place, Switzerland

1995

Gayle purses her fag-crinkled lips. 'He's going,' she says.

'You reckon?' I say.

She nods, blinking slowly.

'How can you tell?'

'It's in his eyes, Con. A look.'

She's talking about Mark. I don't pay any attention. Gayle is forever pursing her fag-crinkled lips and declaring, in a low, knowing voice that so-and-so is on the way out.

'Don't ever listen to Gayle – she's full of shit,' Michelle once told me, when I first started working there in ninety-one.

Mark's got short white hair that pokes out of a skullcap of dandruff and wears glasses as thick as ashtrays. He's around six-foot-tall with a swollen stomach. You can tell he used to have a good body – his shoulders are big and shapely, just like my Simon's – but Mark was never handsome. I've seen the black and white photographs on his dresser. His teeth are too big for his face, a bit like those tortoises from the Creature Comforts adverts. But for what God taketh away, He giveth back: Mark's got a big willy, unlike Ted next door whose penis is so small it lives inside him.

To be honest, Mark is bloody gross. His hearing aids are always clogged with thick brown wax and his nose never stops running. He saves his snottiest sneezes for the dinner table. Evil Audrey, who sits next to him, may not have her marbles anymore but she knows what she likes and it's not snot and gravy.

'You stupid, *stupid* man,' she'll say, her false teeth popping out between words.

Because Mark can't hear her, and because he thinks Audrey is his wife, he places his hand on top of hers and smiles sweetly, as if she's just told him she cherishes him, and always will.

'Mind, you can't blame her,' Michelle will whisper in my ear. 'Turns your stomach, doesn't it?'

It's like there's a plunger inside Mark's body that is very slowly being pushed in, so that all the snot and wax is being pushed out of his orifices like the silly putty spaghetti my boys used to play with.

But I can forgive Mark this because he's an absolute sweetheart. Every time I do something for him – even something as small as brushing cake crumbs from his shirt collar – he gives me a gorgeous big smile and says, 'Faaaahnk yooouu.' Sometimes I get a thumbs up too. It depends on how much energy he has.

He hasn't had a lot of energy lately. I'm so used to seeing him asleep that when he wakes up, blinking behind his massive glasses like a cartoon mole, I feel almost uneasy, as if Lazarus has just twitched a finger.

One week later. Gayle is not the only doomsayer among us. Michelle's saying it. Holly's saying it. Hatima and Vicky are saying it.

I started to believe it on the Tuesday, five-to-nine, when his legs gave way and he fell to the floor, and Holly and I had to carry him to bed, the pair of us moaning the whole time that we're not paid enough to do our backs in (which we are not). I truly believed it when I found him, two mornings in a row, lying on the bedroom floor with his diarrhoea-filled Y-fronts around his knees.

He's going. It won't be long now.

Today it's my job to take his food. Mark's sat in his armchair, one long leg draped over the other, arms crossed. Never one for the telly, he's gazing out of the window. When he sees me he smiles and pops a trembling thumb up. I put the tray on the table in front of him and pick up the fork. Mark shakes his head. He doesn't want to be fed. Not because he's proud, but because he doesn't want to be a burden.

'Don't put yourself out,' he tells me.

'Don't be silly,' I shout. Mark's never a burden. Even when I'm trying to wipe off dried poo from the back of his bollocks he's not a burden.

I sit in the chair opposite his. An *Eldorado* repeat is coming on. 'I'm just going to sit here while you eat,' I shout.

'That's nice,' he says. He stabs a roastie with his fork, pokes it into his mouth and chews with the enthusiasm of a cow. 'Whereabouts in Switzerland are you going?' he says, after swallowing.

'No, Mark. I said I'm going to *sit here* while you eat.'

'It's a beautiful place, Switzerland.'

'No, love! I'm not going to Switzerland!'

'Where will you be staying?'

'Listen. Mark. What I said was…' I let out a sigh. Let the old bugger think I'm off to Switzerland. 'I'm staying near the centre,' I say, not knowing Switzerland from Sarajevo.

'That's nice,' he says.

We settle into silence. Mark eats, then stops. I prompt him to eat more. He eats, then stops. It goes on. Let him take as long as he likes. His hands are shaking, granted, but look at the pluses – he's awake, he's eating and he's making conversation. Turns out Gayle *is* full of shit.

I'm in North Wales for a karate training weekend. Not for myself – God forbid – but for my son Josh, who I'm proud to say is now a brown belt. His father is over the moon – 'My son, the next Bruce Lee,' he likes to joke. We're staying in a log cabin in the forest next to a small, furious river that would eat my toe like a piranha if I dared dip it in. It's beautiful here and I don't even mind that it hasn't stopped raining. Here in the forest it feels like the scenes in *Dirty Dancing* when Johnny takes Baby to learn the jumps.

It's the last night and that is reason enough for me to crack open the wine before it's socially acceptable. Josh is down the clubhouse, playing pool and flirting with the girls most likely, and Simon's taking a nap in the bedroom. Sez, my youngest, is sat cross-legged on the sofa putting stickers in his *Gladiators* sticker book – he's found another boy here who also collects them and they've done their swapsies with the shrewdness of market traders, arguing over the worth of a rare Hunter compared to Night Shade 103. I wish he'd go down the clubhouse with his brother and all the other boys. But of course he thinks they're all idiots. In his own words: 'mongs'. 'If you keep acting like you're better than other people,' I told him earlier, 'then no one will want to be your friend.'

'Good,' he said.

He is in for a rude awakening one day.

I tidy up, hanging up wet gi's and jackets, picking up sparring mitts and empty Lucozade bottles off the floor. I switch the TV on and it's *Stars in Their Eyes*. I can hear men go past the cabin, laughing and shouting – the black belts from Leeds probably, on their way to the clubhouse. A rowdy bunch, they are. Handsome too, though you won't find me telling my Simon that. I put some lasagne in the microwave and pour another glass of wine – a lovely sweet rosé. I lean my elbows on the counter. Two women are doing Shakespeare's Sister.

'They're good, aren't they?' I say to Sez. 'Do you remember when Holly's fella went on as Bryan Ferry?'

He shakes his head without looking up from his sticker book.

'Holly from work. Her husband. You were probably too young to remember.'

'Oh, Mum, that reminds me,' he says, twisting around in his chair. 'I was supposed to pass a message from work.'

'Work?'

'Yeah. They rang when you were packing. They said Mike died in his sleep. Said you'd want to know.'

'Mark.'

'What?'

'Mark, not Mike. And you only just thought to tell me this now? A week later?'

He rolls his eyes. 'I for*got*.'

I sip my wine. I can feel my face tightening. Mark. Lovely old Mark, always said thank you.

I leave the cabin. As soon as the door closes behind me I start crying. The wind whips cold stinging droplets of rain at my face. I won't have him in there see me cry. He'll only use it against me somehow. I walk to the edge of the small river and look down. The water's viciously swirling itself into a brown froth. I go down the little bank that is all mud and tufts of bramble weed. I think about Mark, how he used to point at the photograph of himself tacked to his bedroom door and say, 'Who's that handsome man?' and

I'd always say, 'I dunno, but isn't he *gor*geous?' I think about how I always held his hand because his legs were spaghetti.

Poor lovely Mark. I always take their passing badly but there are a select few who really make an impact and when these go, it can feel like losing an old friend. I make my arms go like airplane wings and tilt my face up to the black sky. I must look like a bloody hippy. I hear kids in the distance, near the parking lot where they've been training all week. Sneaking Thunderbird and Mad Dog 20/20 most likely, copping feels, playing spin the bottle, young and full of that vital something, a heady mix of hope, anger, energy and sex; I remember it well.

The mud starts sliding beneath my feet. I try to get my balance, arms flapping, but it's useless and I fall forward, landing on my stomach and winding myself. I slip down the bank, scraping my skin on thorny weeds and sharp stones. I'm sliding down fast, really bloody fast, heading face first into the wild river. I grab at a thick clump of knotgrass and dig my toes into the mud and jolt to a stop. Hell's bells. Shit. I open my eyes. My nose is inches from the water. Bloody hell. I could've fallen in, bust my skull, drowned, who knows? I could be dead. Holding Mark's hand up there in the clouds, supporting his weight and cracking the same tired jokes over and over again. I claw my way up the bank, wide-eyed and groaning – it's touch and go for a bit; my shoes are slipping in the mud. My forearm, calf and hip are covered in bloody scratches. I'm absolutely filthy with mud.

I feel like a fool. Like a bloody fool. Honouring the passing of a man's life by standing in the rain with my arms out? Bloody stupid. I could've just raised my drink and said, 'To Mark.'

I stagger back into the cabin. Smithy's over. Smithy's fifteen and a black belt already. Him and Josh have bonded this week because they are the only black boys training. Right now he's on the floor, sweaty, topless, doing knuckle push-ups, his young tight muscles bulging like chestnuts. Josh, also topless, is crouched next to him, plenty of boy in his skinny torso, only just beginning to fill out. He's counting every push-up. 'Fifteen-ah …sixteen-ah…seventeen-ah.' Every count is punctuated by a slap to the floor.

'Is that all, son?' Josh says. He is testing out being a man, I can hear it in his voice.

'Just gettin' warmed up,' grunts Smithy, into the carpet. 'Nineteen-ah…twenty! Another twenty to go, bitch!'

I let the door close behind me with a clatter. Both boys look up a little fearfully. They are probably drunk. Josh understands that I've been watching him trying to be a man. I still bring him hot chocolate and biscuits before bed.

'Oh my *God*!' It's Sez. Standing by the fridge. He's looking at me with a hand smacked over his mouth. His eyes are full of nasty laughter. 'What the hell happened to you? You look like the thing from the black lagoon!' He turns to his brother. 'Mum's gotten drunk and fallen in the river!'

I stride up to him and give his face a clean, smart slap.

Snow Angels

1995

And he thought he could get away with it. The destroyed equipment – what's left of it – is scattered on the cement floor. Empty plant pots, feeding tubes, dirty buckets. My Reeboks crunch over smashed light bulbs. The plasterboard walls are intact. Inside there's dusty hose pipes and more buckets. There's a foil-like sheet all ripped up on the floor – some special material that blocks heat, stops the helicopters from seeing. Dad was careful. But dumb at the same time. This is Granddad's garage. His own father's garage. And he thought he could get away with it. The other thing too.

We got the phone call halfway through *Stars in Their Eyes*. Cara answered it. She said, 'Mum, it's Pauline,' and Mum rolled her eyes. She went and sat out the hall, bottom of the stairs, and picked up the novelty Goofy phone.

Pauline was my older sister Shannon's foster parent. I'd only met her once – she had a fat stomach and a huge pair of boobs that looked like one giant boob under her jumper. She looked like a dinnerlady. Her name was Pauline Burger.

Shannon moved out three months ago, just before Halloween. She'd stolen a tenner from our Xmas piggy bank so Mum took away her front door key, grounded her for two weeks and yanked the plug off her television. Shannon went berserk. She called Mum a drug-addict and a hypocrite and said she was leaving. Mum looked at

Shannon through collapsing eyes and said, 'Fine, go and live with your father, see if he'll have you. Go and live with your dear old dad!' So that's what Shannon did.

Dad only had a bedsit. It was crawling with fleas from his Greyhound bitch and Shannon had so many bites on her she looked like she had a disease or something. The social workers didn't think a teenage girl should be living in this place. No privacy, no space, no bed – just a couch covered in fag burns and an old hospital blanket. Also, Dad had the court case coming up and he was probably going to prison for a while.

The social worker arranged for her to live with Pauline Burger. Pauline had a big house in the Heath area. She had three other teenagers living with her – a boy and two girls. She got paid something like three hundred pounds a week for each teenager. When Mum first met her she said, 'That sounds like a pretty sweet deal,' and Pauline shook her head and said, 'It doesn't feel like a sweet deal when you're having to press charges against them for GBH. Or when you find baggies of speed in the butter dish.'

No one's forcing her to do it, are they?

A mechanic from Cardiff was on. 'Tonight Matthew, I'm going to be Bryan Ferry.' I could smell the pizza cooking in the kitchen. Mum came back in. She looked awful. Like her face had been rubbed out by one of those rubbers that don't work properly. She sat down, elbows on her knees.

Cara said, 'What is it?'

Mum said, 'Turn the TV down,' so I did.

'Cara, Polly…I don't know if I should be telling you this.' She looked at the muted television. Bryan Ferry in a bad wig was clutching a microphone, doing sex eyes for the camera.

Cara said, 'Tell us what?'

'This is a bad thing. But you need to hear it. Just in case...just in case.' She stood up and went out the kitchen. I heard hinges crying and a boxy scrabbling. She was in the medicine tub under the sink. I heard running tap water. She came back out, sat in her chair and lit a cigarette.

'Pauline says she found a condom in Shannon's bin. A used condom.' She took a pinched little puff on her cigarette. 'Apparently no one'd been in that room all day. Except your father.'

I looked at Cara, Cara looked at me.

'According to Pauline, your father visited Shannon this evening. He stayed in her room for an hour or so. When he left, Pauline went in with some clean clothes and saw the condom in the bin. It looked fresh.'

She examined our faces with eyes like rusty pennies. And then her cigarette started shaking between her fingers and she was crying. Cara ran over and wrapped an arm round her neck. Mum grabbed Cara's wrist and pulled her down to eye level. She stared into her face and said, 'Cara, baby, has he ever touched you?'

Cara said, 'No! Don't even say that! That's fucking gross.' She sat on the floor and took a cigarette out of Mum's box.

Mum looked at me.

I said, 'Don't even waste your breath.'

Mum nodded then frowned. 'I guess Shannon's always been close to your father.' She looked at the silent television again. Hadn't even noticed her fourteen-year-old daughter smoking her cigarettes right under her nose. 'She was always the Daddy's girl.'

Cara tapped ash into her cupped palm and said, 'Me and Polly were always the tomboys, weren't we?'

Mum nodded. 'And you're twins. Twins are connected. Remember that time with the broccoli? Maybe he wouldn't've taken the risk.' She dropped her head into her hands. 'God. I can't believe I'm even…' She looked up with an expression of sleepy thoughtfulness. 'She was always a bit disturbed, Shannon. Not like you two. Maybe now we know where she gets all her anger from. I can't believe I never—'

I said, 'I think this is bullshit. It's probably that Assim. Not fucking *Dad*.'

Assim was the boy who lived in Pauline's house. He was a skinny Indian who smoked spliffs like cigarettes. I'd met him once. He wore a big black puffer jacket and a gold chain. He was miserable and mean. Shannon said it was because he was an orphan and no one'd ever loved him.

'I wish it *was* Assim. But when Pauline questioned Shannon she said it wasn't.'

I rolled my eyes. 'Oh, come on. She's lying. It's against house rules.'

'But wouldn't she prefer people to think she was sleeping with Assim than her own—God, I can't even say it.' She stubbed out her fag, almost missing the ashtray. 'I said the same thing to Pauline. I said, "Now come on now, Pauline, I know Shannon. She's not gunna let people think she's… you know," and Pauline says, "Well, when I suggested that it might be her father, Shannon had this guilty look."' Mum looked at the pair of us with a tired matter-of-factness. 'First the drugs and now this. If your father has done this…thing, I will kill him. I will stab his eyes out of his face.'

Cara said, 'This is dark as fuck,' and Mum nodded.

We went quiet. Just the whispery *puh* of puckered lips taking nips of nicotine, the sizzle of the paper burning down. The ticking clock hand. Then the sound of the oven pinging.

Mum said, 'Pizza's done.'

101

I knock on the plasterboard with my knuckles. Behind me is Dad's red Renault hatchback. It's been here since the divorce, next to Granddad's old bicycle frames. Dad was planning to sell it. He was going to change a couple of tyres, get it MOTd, advertise in *Free Ads*. But he won't be able to do that now, not where he is. Twelve months for growing weed. I wonder what he's doing now. Sat in his cell? Watching TV from his bunk bed?

The day after Pauline's phone call, Mum rang up Dad to confront him about the condom in the bin. He went very quiet. Mum listened to his nose-breathing and said, 'Well what have you got to say for yourself?' with a voice that could stab through bone. He said, 'I can't believe you would think that, Liz,' and hung up.

Mum was left with silence, the not-funny-anymore Goofy phone in her fist. Pauline, who had come over that morning, stood in the hall listening to the conversation. She said, 'You'd think he'd fight his corner more than that, wouldn't you? If that was me and I was innocent I'd be furious. I'd be talking about slander.'

Mum said, 'He's bloody guilty. I just know it.'

Dad never fought his corner. Kept horribly silent. Shannon was the same. She ripped through the house like an angry mute when she needed food and the bathroom, according to Pauline, but the rest of the time she stayed in her bedroom with the cordless telephone ('Calling who?' said Pauline. 'Her father?').

And she wouldn't say who it was. Would not say who it was.

Pauline said, 'I always thought he was creepy. So quiet. And the way he just stares.'

Mum popped a tablet from one of her blister packs and drank it down with her black coffee. 'At least he'll be in prison soon.'

'Yes, but not for the reason he should be.' Pauline dipped a coconut ring in her tea and let it collapse into her mouth. 'If he went inside for screwing his daughter, the other prisoners would rip him a new you-know-what.'

And Mum burst into tears. It was that word, I think. Screwing.

There's a box of tapes in the corner of the garage. Dad's tapes. Rolling Stones, *Satanic Majesties*; Cream, *Wheels of Fire*; Blur, *Parklife* (he'd bought this last one because he wanted to know what all the fuss was about – I told him he was better off going with Oasis but he didn't like what they said about being bigger than the Beatles). I upend the box and all the tapes clatter to the floor. I stamp on them, grind my heel into the plastic casing. It feels good. I rip out all the tape ribbon rolls until I'm surrounded by huge tangles of it.

I go over to the plasterboard box room. This is where all the growing happened. 'Just weed,' Cara had said to me once, in one of her weaker moments. 'It's not like he was making heroin.' I punch through the board. My fist sinks in easily, making a messy hole, a small explosion. Chalk dust sprinkles my trainers. I do it again a few inches over. Paper and chunks of chalk everywhere, a nice throbbing in my knuckles. I keep doing it. Sometimes I don't punch hard enough and my fist just thuds the thick board. But I keep going. I remember when Dad started going to kyokushinkai classes. He'd come home and start doing knuckle push-ups on breeze blocks to harden his fists. I did them beside him, a scrawnier, girl-shaped version, just thirteen, on house bricks instead of breeze blocks. I wanted to be as strong as him.

I run out of places to punch. I grab a piece of chalk from the floor and scrawl 'PERVERT' on the timber that supports the board. I kick some paint tins over: creamy Magnolia seeps and spreads; Twilight Cinders splatters in silky grey-purple ribbons. I pick up a hammer leaning against the cobwebbed far wall and smash the windows of Dad's Renault with it. The glass spiderwebs then implode and scatter. I kick the side mirrors till they hang by their wires, I hammer the headlights. Then I start on the bodywork. The dusty old garage is so filled with clanging I almost expect the walls to collapse, like the shout that starts off an avalanche.

I toss the hammer away and just stand there for a while. I feel good. I let my breathing get back to normal and then I leave the garage and walk up the garden path toward the house, where Nana is making Welsh cakes in the kitchen.

Dad wrote me and Cara a letter from prison. A note really. 'I don't know what to say to you both accept its not true about Shannon and I love you very much. One day you will know this. I hope your studying hard at school and looking out for each other. Dad. xxx' We burnt it out the garden with Mum's long oven matches. We did it at night in silence surrounded by a circle of candles. We'd watched *The Craft* recently and Cara was dressed like Nancy, in a dog collar and thick eyeliner. We also burnt photographs of him and gifts he'd given us last Christmas – Miss Selfridges bum-bags, signed pictures of Brian Harvey from East 17. The next day we rang Pauline's house and Shannon answered. I said, 'Why don't you just admit it?' and she hung up.

But did it matter? Knowing, not knowing. What fucking difference did it make? Something ugly had grown out of my young life, tearing through it like nettles. That was all that mattered.

It's a crunchy kind of snow and almost five inches deep. I tread through it in a pair of Dr Martens. Crunch, crunch. Cold fog blasts out of my mouth. I swipe snow off the tops of cars until my hands are almost mauve. I stop outside the creepy old care home and peer in through the front window, staring at all the miserable old people in armchairs, most of them asleep. A carer comes into the room and I run away, kicking up snow. I turn into Leopold Park. It's empty except two people sitting on the swings. Two dark dots lost in the white dunes. A girl and a boy, kissing. I get closer. Shannon and Assim. His black bomber jacket and weak-coffee skin, her long red hair and army surplus coat.

I start running and they whip their heads toward me. Shannon's face is spotty. I stick my hands out and shove her off the swing and she lands hard. I throw myself on her. I punch her nose and blood sprays out. Something cracks inside my hand, a bone or something. I feel fingers scrape my scalp and then a jolting agony. Assim yanks me backwards by my hair then lets go. Two sisters on their backs in the snow. Looks like we're making snow angels.

Assim says, 'What the fuck are you doing?'

I ignore him. I sit up. 'Why did you let people think that about Dad?' I shout at Shannon. She's still lying in the snow. 'How could you let us *think* that, you stupid bitch?'

Shannon sits up groggily. Blood and snot coming out of her nose. She wipes it and looks at the glove. 'You've broken my nose, you fucking mental bitch!'

'Yeah? I'll do more than that.' I try to sit up but Assim puts one Nike Air on my chest and firmly pushes me back down. I thump his shin. 'Get the fuck off me, you fucking Paki!'

Tutting with snarled lips, he takes his foot away and I sit back up. My hand is starting to hurt bad. 'Why didn't you tell us the truth, Shannon?'

'Because I would've been kicked out! Because I liked it there and Pauline would've kicked me out and I was fucking scared!'

'So? I'd rather sleep in the streets than have people think I was fucking my own father.'

Shannon gets up, crinkling her nose, testing the pain. 'Well you didn't *have* to think that, did you? You didn't *have* to jump to that conclusion.' She stands over me. 'Just leave me alone. You and Mum and fucking Tweedledee.' She takes Assim's hand. 'And don't call him a Paki. I didn't think you were like that, Polly.'

And she walks off.

I sit on the swing, cradling my clawed-up hand. I look at the blood in the snow and think nasty thoughts. Kick it until it goes crystal-pink like a drained Slush Puppy.

A Peacock is a Good Thing

2007

There they were again. Four cigarettes rattling around a packet. Richmond Superkings. Marv took one out and slipped it behind his ear. He sniffed the box, smiling, and put it in his pocket. This was the sixth Saturday in a row. Always four cigarettes in a Richmond pack. Always in the postbox on the corner of Tarleton Avenue and at the top of the sack, which meant they'd probably been dropped in the night before or in the early hours of the morning.

He tied up the sack and heaved it into the back of his van. He heard a loud, drawn out cat's cry come from somewhere in the distance – the other end of Tarleton Avenue it sounded like. *Myyyyeeeeeeeeooooo*. He'd heard the cry the last two mornings, a stray cat stuck in a tree maybe. Not his problem. He locked the postbox, leaned against it and pulled out the fag from behind his ear, lighting it with a match. When he'd found the first lot of cigarettes six weeks ago, he'd been suspicious and thrown them away. The second lot he was even more suspicious. Someone trying to poison the postman? Silly? Probably. But it could happen. The third lot he'd given to Frank Marsden who worked on the Rhiwbina route.

The next day in the sorting office, Frank was his normal self, whistling off-key tunes through lips that looked like a dog's arsehole and telling the temp staff a joke about rape. So the cigarettes were fine. Marv smoked the fourth lot himself. He chose to see them as a gift. They tasted better than his own cigarettes even though they were the same brand.

The fifth time it happened the fag box smelled faintly like perfume. Fruity with a bit of vanilla, like the scent Julie used to wear.

He imagined her as a natural redhead with bright blue eyes and a big arse. A cleavage you could lose your keys in. But she could look like anything. She might look like Fat Betty who lived on Ismail-Enver Close. Forty stone of clammy flesh dripping over the sides of a mobility scooter. She might look like Miss S Childs who lived above the drum shop on Godfrey-Bouillon Road. Huge sausage nose, the kind you want to twang like a diving board. Some kind of hormone imbalance: more hair on her chin than on her head.

But she might be a redhead with blue eyes.

Marv got in his van, tuned the radio to Classic Rock FM, and drove to the next postbox.

She could be anything.

The next morning as Marv delivered letters, he had a thought. Maybe the cigarettes were meant for *him*. It kind of made sense. Richmond Superkings were his brand. The Tarleton Avenue pick-up on Saturday morning was his pick-up. Maybe some woman saw him buying fags at the off-licence over the road. Saw him and liked him.

He laughed bitterly at this, surprising a passing woman and her child. He was old with permanent grey stubble. His teeth were terrible. His mouth turned down at the corners and drooped. He looked like a sad clown without any make-up on – someone had actually told him that though he couldn't remember who. What woman would ever like him?

Someone desperate, he thought, slamming a letter through a thin bronze mailbox. Someone like Fat Betty.

He caught his reflection in the beaded glass of the front door. It was dark, just a silhouette. He went out the front gate and looked in the side mirror of a parked car. The tired brown eyes, the broken nose, the curved white scar cutting through his chin fuzz. He smiled, showing his teeth. They were like pegs burnt at the edges. The rest wasn't so bad. He looked rough, like he'd had a hard life, but he wasn't ugly exactly.

Didn't some women like rough old guys? Yes, some did. Girls too. Girls with daddy issues. Back when he was forty-seven, he'd had an affair with a plump young thing called Jane and she'd called him Old Grizzly Bollocks and run her hand through his grey chest fuzz like it was a golden fleece, and though she never did admit it, she'd loved him.

He went up Yahya-Khan Avenue followed by Hideki Tojo Avenue – these streets, from what he'd heard, were named after nineteenth century Asian tycoons who'd been buddies of the Marquis of Bute. Frank Marsden liked to call this area the Slit-Eye Quarter. When he got to Hirohito Avenue, it struck him: why the *four* cigarettes? What was the significance? Could it be code? Maybe she was trying to tell him her address? Four Richmond Road? That seemed possible. Richmond Road was a ten-minute walk from the postbox. Certainly it was possible. If a little far-fetched.

A sort of sign? A premonition? Four cigarettes. Four years until he contracted lung cancer and died. A message from beyond the grave. From Julie. *You know what smoking does to people, you saw what it did to me.*

Silly hocus-pocus. Besides, Julie had never been one to fanny-arse about like that – she was a straight shooter. She'd show up at the end of his bed at the stroke of midnight and say, 'Stop smoking, you stupid dickhead.' That was his Julie.

109

He finished his round at midday. He drove home to his bedsit, had a shave, second of the day, and made himself a cup of tea. He sat in his chair in silence, sipping at his drink. He thought of Julie. He put on *Eggheads* and half-watched it. Maybe the woman wouldn't be a beautiful redhead. Maybe she would just be nice-looking. He imagined holding hands with a *nice*-looking woman. Christmas shopping, long walks through the woods in winter, feet crunching snow and ice.

He had another cup of tea – his last of the day (he only ever had the two), then he made himself beans and sausages on toast. Ruined it with too much salt, ate it anyway.

The postbox was outside a hair salon called Kadji Hair, just on the corner of Tarleton Avenue, a small tree-lined street of terraced houses. Marv was sitting on Kadji's step, wearing his winter coat. You could get bone-cold if you sat still for too long, even in the spring. At his feet was a tall Thermos full of strong, sweet coffee. He sat and smoked, his portable radio tuned to Planet Rock. It was eleven o'clock at night. Clusters of students wobbled by picking at loaded kebabs and shouting at each other good-naturedly. Some loners steamed past, hands stuffed in pockets.

By now the woman looked like Melinda Messenger but well seasoned. She was a pub landlady. She had gentle ways but she challenged him. They had already had their first argument, followed by rough sex against a wall. She liked the taste of jizz. Genuinely liked it. She made a great Sunday roast.

He took a sandwich out of his bag, egg salad, and ate it, leaving the crusts for tomorrow's seagulls. He went for a piss behind a parked van around the corner. He heard a cat's cry – *Myyyyyyeeeeeee*. Someone needed to do something about that damned cat, wherever it was. He wasn't a great lover of cats but he didn't like the idea of one stuck somewhere in pain, lonely, calling out, and no one doing anything about it.

At two-twenty a broad woman in a tiger stripe mackintosh dropped a small metallic blue box into the postbox.

Marv stood up. 'Hey!'

The woman glanced over her shoulder at him and carried on walking.

'Hey! Hang on.'

She walked faster.

He ran after her. She spun round. 'What? What do you want?'

He saw her scared old face, lit up by lamplight, and his dreams unravelled.

'What is it?' Her eyes skittered over the empty road and pavement. '*What?*'

'Sorry to frighten you, sorry.' He showed her his palms – no weapons. 'You dropped some fags in the postbox.'

She looked at the postbox. Then back to him. 'So?'

'So I'm the postman. I've been – sorry, I feel really stupid now – I've been wondering who's been dropping the fags in the postbox. It's been driving me crazy.'

She laughed, incredulous, her mascara-caked lashes flapping. 'The postman?'

Marv nodded. 'I know it sounds stupid.'

She shook her head. 'No, it's – no, it's just bloody weird.' She gave him a baffled smile. 'Why do you *think* I've been leaving the fags then?'

He shrugged. 'No idea.'

'You must've had a theory.'

He shook his head. 'Nope.'

Again, the baffled smile. The woman was middle-aged. Fifties maybe. She had short bleached hair with brown bits in it, large green eyes with saggy, hooded lids and cobwebs of laughter lines – sooty black eyeliner had smudged and got into the creases. Her face was heavily powdered, her mouth smeared with fuchsia pink lipstick that gleamed like PVC. She had jowls.

'I better put you out of your misery then,' she said. 'I quit smoking recently, but I like a fag when I drink. And every Friday I meet up with my sister for a few voddies. I buy a pack of ten, I drink six double vodkas and Coke throughout the night and I have a fag with each one. And on the way home I drop the leftover fags into the postbox, so I'm not tempted to smoke any more. See?'

'But why the postbox?'

'I dunno. I never stopped to consider what the postman would think!' She laughed, deeply, huskily, nose crinkling, front teeth flashing. She had nice teeth, Marv noticed. Or dentures. 'I would've preferred to give them to a homeless person but there's never any around when you want one. So I chucked them in the postbox. Good a place as any.' She laughed again, slapping a hot-pink-tipped hand on his forearm. 'And there you were, trying to figure it all out.'

He smiled. 'Yes. I was.' He looked her up and down. She was built like a fridge, big and solid from the shoulders to the hips. Huge breasts that swelled out of her coat, the skin on her throat red and sun-damaged. Thin, shapely legs ending in strappy heels.

'And you've been sitting out here all blinking night?'

He nodded.

'You poor sod. You must be freezing. You get home to your bed.'

'Chance would be a fine thing. I've got work in a bit.'

112

'You haven't!'

He nodded, grimly.

'Oh dear.' She drawstringed her lips and looked at him. 'Why don't you come back to mine? You can sit in front of the fire for a bit.'

'Um.' He looked at his watch for too long.

'Don't worry, I'm not going to maul you.'

He laughed, nervously. 'I know, I know.' Laughed again. 'OK. I will. Thanks.'

He went and got his flask and radio and empty sandwich wrappers. They turned off Tarleton Avenue onto Haile Mariam Avenue.

'I'm Pauline,' she said. 'Pauline Burger.'

'Marvin,' he said. 'Call me Marv.'

'Nice to meet you, Marv.'

'And you.'

She lived at fifty Haile Mariam Avenue. Marv recognised the door.

'Mrs P Stefanakis,' he said.

'You clever man,' she said, twisting the key in the lock. 'Course, I'm not Stefanakis anymore. Gone back to my maiden name. Not for the first time.' The front door swung open. She reached inside, fumbled around, and the landing light came on. A fat white cat ran to meet her.

'Mummy's home!' She bent down to pet it. 'Hello, Munchkin.' Then a fat tortoiseshell ambled over, followed by a fluffy black cat so obese Marv laughed out loud.

Pauline peered at him from over her shoulder, eyes twinkling. 'I know – fat as hell. It's cuz they have cat flu. I don't feed them too much or anything.'

'They're bloody massive.'

She nodded. 'You're not wrong there, Mister Postman.'

She took off her coat and hung it up. She had on a little black dress that clung to her giant bosom and each stomach roll. He hung his coat up and took his shoes off. There was a hole in the big toe of his sock. He curled his toes under to hide them. She led him into the living room and turned the electric fire on. It was a cosy-looking room; scuffed beige leather settee, colourful Indian rugs, multi-coloured fake-fur cushions, glass ornaments and cat figurines everywhere, an antique Welsh dresser. In the corner there was a well-polished piano and hanging above it, a black and white film poster of Paul Newman and Elizabeth Taylor in *Cat on a Hot Tin Roof*. On the windowsill, a cactus bulged out of its pot like a limb with elephantiasis. An out-of-place games console on the floor in front of the TV, Playstation or Xbox or whatever they were called.

Marv smiled politely and hovered near the settee.

'Have a seat,' she said.

He sat down.

'Drink?'

'Please.'

'Tea? Or something stronger?'

'Well. I shouldn't really.'

'A sherry?'

He nodded.

She went out and came back with two drinks. She put a CD on. Dusty Springfield. She sat down opposite him, crossing one leg over the other. The white cat rubbed its face against her shin.

'Have you been hearing that cat lately?' Marv asked.

Pauline looked at him blankly.

'I can hear it some mornings, near Tarleton Avenue. Sounds like a cat stuck up a tree.'

'Oh that,' she said. She leaned forward with this look in her eyes like she was about to divulge something wicked. 'It's not a cat, it's a peacock.'

'What?'

Her eyes gleamed. 'I know, that's what I thought when I found out. A peacock, you've got to be kidding me? What I've been told is a man down the road bought a peacock – actually bought a peacock, I know – and it got loose. I said to my sister – she's the one who told me about it, I said, "Well, what did he *think* would happen, the daft sod?"' She sipped her drink then wiped the corner of her mouth with her thumb. 'It's been loose a week now, though I've never seen it. I can hear it though – it kept me up all bloody night the first time. It's not hurt, apparently, it's its mating call. Fancy that though – buying a peacock.'

'Now I've heard everything,' said Marv, smiling. 'Is it OK if I smoke?'

'Course. Mind if I have one? Seeing as I'm still drinking?'

'Sure. I'll be getting four more later on, won't I?'

They laughed. He lit a fag and passed her one. Dusty sang 'The Windmills of Your Mind'. The other two cats came in and twined their plump bodies around Pauline's legs.

'You know, this is a very peculiar situation,' said Pauline.

'It is.' The fattest cat came over to him. He sat forward and stroked it behind the ears.

They sat in silence for a while, sipping their drinks.

'So,' said Marv. 'Where's Mr Stefanakis? Not that I'm – ya know.'

'I know.' She breathed out smoke through her nostrils. 'Mr Stefanakis is currently living with a dental nurse half his age.'

'Oh. Sorry to hear that.'

'Oh, it's OK. Mr Stefanakis was a bastard to be honest, Marv. A complete bastard. I'm well rid.' She examined the orange tip of her cigarette. 'Lovely things, cigarettes. I do miss them.' She looked up at Marv. 'How about you? Married?'

Marv shook his head. 'Widowed.'

'Oh, that's terrible!'

He nodded. 'Cancer. Uterine.'

'You poor man. I can't begin to understand how that feels.'

Marv shrugged a little. 'You get used to it. Well, you try to.'

The song changed. Pauline went and got more drinks. They started talking about their lives. Pauline was an ex-psychiatric nurse, used to work in that care home near Leopold Park, before it got turned into a care home, back when it housed mentally ill people ('though by all accounts it still does, only they're a lot older and they need Zimmer frames – oh, I'm awful!'). Lasted sixteen years in the job. Left after the third stabbing attempt. The last twenty years she'd been fostering teenagers, had three of them at the moment, all girls, 'a real handful, never mind all that sugar and spice and all things nice rubbish'; right now they were in Llangrannog for the weekend, riding horses and God knows what else. It was tough, fostering, really bloody tough, but rewarding too. Her sister was her best friend. She adored animals. She loved to go dancing – oh, she just loved it – but didn't get the opportunity these days, what with her demanding wards and lack of men friends. She'd been divorced twice. The first husband embezzled her money and sold all her antique furniture, except the Welsh dresser and piano. Family heirlooms. The scoundrel. She was sixty-one.

Marv told her about his job. There wasn't much to tell.

116

He'd never been bitten by a dog. He got rained on a lot. There was talk about Royal Mail modernising and downsizing. He'd gone on strike twice in the past year. His workmates ranged from 'all right' to 'bloody ignorant.' But the job was fine really. He'd never been the ambitious sort. A decent wage, a place to live and some good songs on the radio, that was all he wanted ('and a woman', he almost said). He had a grown-up son, Gareth, but they rarely saw each other. Not because they'd argued or anything. They were just both terrible at keeping in touch.

After their third drink Pauline did something irregular. She was talking about her sister's violent husband when she paused suddenly, leaned over to one side and let out a loud fart. 'Pardon me,' she said, flapping her hand. And then she went back to talking about her sister's husband. As if it had never happened. Or she just didn't care.

Marv pretended to listen but really his mind was on the fart. 'Women don't do that,' he thought. 'Julie never did that. Not when I was around.' He didn't know if he should be disgusted or impressed. 'It's refreshing, I suppose,' he thought. Maybe Pauline was a free spirit?

At ten to five, Pauline brought in a plate of nibbles. Cheese on crackers, crisps, cashew nuts. She poured Marv another sherry. He was starting to feel good. He was thinking about calling in sick. 'I Only Want to Be with You' came on. Pauline kicked her shoes off and started dancing, eyes closed, lips moving to the words, bare feet tapping and swishing, flabby arms waving about lazily.

Marv watched her, hand running up and down the white cat's back. She closed her eyes and smiled at the ceiling. 'Oh, Dusty, you wonderful thing, you.'

Marv pointed at the piano with his cigarette. 'Do you play?'

She flapped a hand. 'Hardly. I had lessons when I was growing up.'

'Play something for me.'

'God no. I'd give you a headache.'

'Don't be silly, love. Go on. Even if it's just Incy Wincy Spider.'

She rolled her smiling eyes. 'Oh, go on then, but don't say I didn't warn you.' She went and turned off the CD player and sat at the piano, her back to Marv. She flipped the lid up. 'Should be in tune.' She turned and looked at him. 'This is a bloody expensive piano, Merv – sorry, *Marv*. It's a Bechstein. You'd never know it from the way I talk, but I was brought up in Cyncoed.' She turned back to the piano. Then back to Marv. 'We had a cleaner, ya know. Very la-dee-da. But I went and married beneath me, didn't I?' She turned back and sorted through a pile of sheet music on top of the piano. Marv got up and stood next to her. 'La Plus Que Lente', Debussy. He'd never heard of it. She relaxed her shoulders and started playing, her hands moving up and down the keys like drunken spiders.

She played wonderfully. The notes tinkled out both serene and sporadic, and Marv closed his eyes. A cigarette hung out of his crescent mouth. Chalky-grey tendrils of smoke drifted up, puffed out, dispersed. Through the window, the black of night was slowly diffusing to grainy twilight. By the time Pauline finished the song the stars had gone.

'Pauline. That was bloody lovely.'

She stood up abruptly, knocking over the stool, and ran out of the room crying.

Marv stood still for a long while. He didn't know what to do. What had upset her? He lifted the stool up and pushed it back into place. Played the highest note with a heavy finger.

She was out the back garden, a hand pressed over her eyes. There were a dozen small cat turds in various stages of decay scattered around the patio, soggy, decaying dandelions slumping their heads, small thick-black spiders coming out from under scraggly mops of weeds. It was light out now.

He wrapped an arm around her and looked down into her face. Waiting for her to fold into his embrace, that's how it was supposed to go. But she just stood there, her pink-tipped hand hiding her eyes, the hand shaking a little. 'What's wrong, love?' he whispered.

She shook her head.

'OK. You don't need to tell me. Only, was it me?'

Another silent shake of the head. She sniffed.

'OK.' He just stood there, his arm feeling awkward now, wrapped around her like that, but fearful that taking it away would only increase the awkwardness.

He felt like someone was watching him. He often had this feeling. He would think, only half-seriously, that it was Julie, her ghost, keeping an eye on him. He glanced over his shoulder. There was a peacock standing on the wall a few feet away. A bloody great peacock. Looking at him, its bright blue head perfectly still.

It's a sign, he thought.

He looked at it. It looked at him. They didn't move. He wanted to tell Pauline to look – Now don't make any sharp movements, he'd say, whispering, but I've just seen something that'll cheer you right up. But he didn't want the spell broken.

It *felt* like a sign. A big, beautiful peacock, watching them from above like some benevolent deity. It couldn't be a bad thing. A vulture – now, that would be a bad thing. A crow with red eyes. A magpie, just the one. Not a peacock. A peacock was a good thing.

The peacock bobbed its head and the movement was like a gulp. A few smaller feathers near the back of its tail fanned out like utensils on a Swiss Army Knife.

One of Pauline's cats came out. Saw the bird. It got ready to spring, its fat haunches down. The peacock clumsily ran along the top of the wall and flew in a Technicolor burst onto next door's roof. It ran along the guttering, a streak of electric blue, disappeared.

Renée Zellweger's Stupid Fucking Smile

2010

It was in the queue for the taxi they met the sisters.

'What happened to your face, chick?' said the one in the dress, her grey eyes huge.

'Fuckin' bouncer,' said Gareth.

'Now there's a surprise,' said the one in the trousers. 'Bastards, the lot of them.'

The one in the dress was done up like a Barbie doll and had what appeared to be silicon implants in her breasts. Gareth noticed Jimmy staring at them from under his thick black lashes. The other wore skinny jeans with red trainers. She had on less make-up than her sister and her chest was almost flat. Both spoke with a gentle northern English accent, though Gareth couldn't pinpoint the specific region. Oop in *Coronation Street* land, his dad would have said.

'Why'd he go and do that for?' said the one in the dress.

'No reason,' said Gareth. 'Look.' He showed them the fleshy gap in his teeth.

'Christ on a bike,' said Trousers.

Dress raised a hand to her mouth – she had red nails – and slowly shook her head. 'Go to the pigs, mate.'

Gareth spat out air. 'Yeah, that's likely.'

Jimmy offered the two girls cigarettes. 'Jimmy,' he said. 'And that's Gareth.'

'Gareth Moon,' said Gareth. He was very proud of his surname.

'Mr Moon. I like it. You should come with us to this house party.'

'Yeah?' said Gareth. 'Where's it to?'

Jimmy looked at him, cross. 'Who gives a fuck where? Let's go.'

The one in the dress was called Simone, named, she said, after the French feminist, Simone de Beauvoir, who believed that a woman is not born a woman, but becomes one. 'And she's Hélène,' she said, pointing to her sister. 'She's named after Hélène Cixous, this French bird who reckoned women should piss standing up.' She explained that their mother had been an ardent academic feminist and activist in her youth, but had grown so bitter about gender inequality that she'd gone on antidepressants and now refused to watch any telly or read any books that might spark her off.

'She wasn't happy about these, I can tell you,' said Simone, pointing at her breasts (Jimmy's eyes eagerly following her fingers). 'She went mental,' said Hélène. 'She thinks we're rebelling against her. I'm getting mine done soon as well. Fuck her.'

'How can a woman piss standin' up?' said Gareth, from the back of the taxi.

'Oh, it can be done,' said Hélène. 'It's just you end up dribbling down your leg.'

'Classy.'

Simone stretched over Jimmy's lap and slapped Gareth on the arm. 'Oi. Don't tell me you've never tucked yer knob between your legs like whassisface outta *Silence of the Lambs*? Whassis-name? Buffalo Bill. And then danced around in the mirror?'

'Fuck off I have,' said Gareth.

Jimmy leaned forward and sniffed the back of Simone's neck.

They were on a neat street lined with cherry blossom trees. Gareth knew the area vaguely: as a kid he'd been forced to visit his great-grandmother in the gloomy care home down the road. Simone and Hélène walked to the end of the block arm in arm, Jimmy and Gareth following. Jimmy was looking at their arses. He'd been joking about blue balls this last week, telling Gareth that he was afraid his cock was going to fall off (he always called it his 'cock'). Gareth would much prefer to be at home now with a kebab. He'd never had much luck convincing women they were onto a good thing with him. He'd stumbled into his last relationships by accident.

Simone turned back and said, 'Now don't blame us if this turns out to be a squat full of crusty hippies, OK?' and Jimmy raised his hands up, as if to say, wouldn't dream of it. They got to the last house and kicked open the garden gate. There was a black Mercedes parked in the driveway. It had flat tyres and the window on the driver's side was sealed up with bin liner. The house was big. Distant bass drifted out of the open front door.

Inside it was mostly empty, but the hundreds of cans and bottles laid out like a miniature metropolis spoke of previous revelry. The living room was dark save for a few strings of fairy lights. A set of decks left abandoned played a jagged psy-trance song. A trashed-looking girl with fluorescent orange dreadlocks stood in the middle of the room swaying to the music, her eyes closed, while an old-ish man with a scruffy auburn beard watched her lovingly, a flagon of cider on his lap. A boy with thick black glasses sat on his knees in the middle of the floor staring up at the ceiling like it was made of snakes.

There were five other rooms in the house, a couple of them empty, the rest filled with clusters of people. They went to the busiest room and sat in a free space on the floor. Jimi Hendrix playing on the cheap CD player in the corner. Gareth found a half-empty bottle of Bud and took a sip. It was warm. Jimmy rested his back on the cold radiator and lit a fag. When he looked up, Simone and Hélène were gone.

'Where'd they go?' he said.

'Lookin' for pills, maybe?'

'They could've said somethin'.'

Jimmy stared at the floor, his brows knotted. Gareth finished the Bud and found a bottle of pear cider with only a few sips missing.

Jimmy stood up. 'Be back in a minute. Piss.' And he left.

Gareth looked around with cool, hopeful eyes. The people here, they weren't the sort who wore fresh-ironed white shirts and went to O'Neills and Walkabout on a Saturday night. Jimmy had a lip piercing and wore Converse trainers so he could sort of fit in anywhere. Gareth looked down at his own feet – tan square-toed leather shoes (Gucci), immaculately polished. A man with flesh tunnels the size of two-pound coins came over. 'Um, I think that's my friend's drink you've got there?'

Gareth lifted the pear cider. 'This?'

The man nodded.

'Nah,' said Gareth. 'I brought this.' He stood up with clicking knee-joints and walked out.

The room was empty except for a young guy sat cross-legged on the bed playing a video game.

'Whassat you're playin' there?'

The boy looked up. He was small-built and good-looking with smooth light-brown skin and an ice-blue quiff. 'Resident Evil.'

'Which one?'

'Four.'

Gareth came all the way in, lifting his drink. 'Excellent.' He sat on the bed next to the boy and watched the gameplay. 'Ah, not that prick with the chainsaw,' he said.

'Yeah. He's killed me, like, twenty times now.' The boy's accent was vaguely Cardiff, his tone sarcastic.

'Want me to have a go?'

The boy passed Gareth the controller and watched him intently as he played.

'Ah, fuck fuck fuck,' said Gareth, yanking the pad around in the direction his character was moving, his blood-crusted mouth hanging open.

The boy went on watching him. He had a small smile on his lips.

'Ah, crap, I'm dead. Sorry.'

'That's OK.' The boy reached under the bed and pulled out a CD covered in small neat rows of white powder. 'Want some?'

Gareth clamped a hand on the boy's sinewy upper arm. 'Bless you, child.'

They did a line each and sat there sniffing.

'So you live here?' said Gareth.

'Nah. I just fancied a party.'

'Is that why you're sat on your own playing video games?'

The boy laughed. 'What happened to your mouth?' he asked.

'Bouncer hit me.'

'Really?' The boy pressed his finger down on one nostril

and sniffed hard. Swallowed, grimaced. 'Bouncers can be bastards.'

'You're tellin' me.' Gareth lifted his lip and showed him the missing tooth.

The boy winced. 'Bastards.' He lit a cigarette. 'What's your name then?'

'Gareth. Gareth Moon.'

'Like Alfie Moon from *EastEnders*.'

Gareth nodded. 'My Dad's name is Marvin Moon. I'm well jealous of his name to be fair.'

'Isn't that a cartoon character?' He tapped ash into an empty coke can. 'No, wait – that's Marvin the Martian. Who'd you come with?'

'My mate Jimmy. And these two sisters. Simone and – what was it? Helena or Ellen or something.'

'Skinny and blonde?' said the boy. 'One of them with big tatas?'

'Yeah, that's them.'

The boy smiled. 'That's Laura and Imogen, that is.'

Gareth shook his head. 'No. They said—'

'They were having you on. They like to make shit up and put on fake accents. They're not even sisters. They're fucking mental.'

Gareth placed a solemn hand on his chest. 'I feel like my whole life up until this point has been a lie.' They laughed together.

The boy was a hairdresser. A 'colour specialist'. Liked it, most of the time, but didn't want to do it forever. Gareth told him about his job fitting smoke detectors, how it brought in the money but he couldn't see himself doing it forever either. His dream was to open a bar in Ibiza. One with a pool table and Sky Sports.

They moved on to favourite bands (the boy rolled his

eyes when Gareth mentioned Coldplay – 'I should have guessed'), *The X Factor*, David Cameron, hallucinogenics, Jesus, islamophobia, adult cartoons, Cadbury's Cream eggs, Renée Zellweger's 'stupid fucking smile', testicular cancer.

They talked about their fear of death. Not so much death itself but *premature* death. Lying in a hospital bed shot full of morphine and fading away at the age of forty. Gareth told the boy that his own mother had died like that, of uterine cancer, and it was the darkest, saddest time of his life so far. He admitted that the future terrified him. Everything terrified him. What if nothing ever happened to him? What if he never fell in love or started a successful career? What if he failed at life and ended up alone? Just some sad old bastard eating microwave meals in front of *A Touch of Frost*, just counting down the years till he was carted off to a depressing nursing home. The boy went quiet. Contemplative. He said he feared the same thing, that everybody does, you'd be an imbecile not to. Gareth leaned in and told him that he used to wet the bed up until the age of nine. 'At least you don't shit the bed,' said the boy, smiling. 'Silver lining.'

Gareth went and found a sticky bottle of red Aftershock in the main room, under the deserted mixing decks. He didn't see Jimmy anywhere. He shared the Aftershock with the boy, who had removed his t-shirt, revealing a set of turquoise wings tattooed on his shoulder blades.

'Nice ink,' said Gareth.

The boy smiled shyly. 'You got any?'

Gareth rolled up his shirtsleeve. He had a Tasmanian devil holding a leek on his porky bicep. The boy ran his forefinger along its surface. 'Cool.'

'Nah, it's shite. I was pissed.'

The boy laughed. 'Yeah, I didn't wanna say.' He looked

at Gareth. Then he quickly darted his head forward like a hen pecking grain, and pressed his lips against Gareth's.

'Whoa there! Whoa!' Gareth snapped his head back like he'd been slapped. 'Fuck!'

The boy sat up straight, closed his eyes and pressed a hand over his mouth. 'I'm sorry,' he said, eventually.

'I'm not that way,' said Gareth.

'I'm sorry.' The boy kept his eyes closed.

Gareth blew out air. 'Fuck.' He downed some Aftershock.

The boy lifted his other hand and covered his face. His naked shoulders started to shake.

Gareth winced. 'Oh, now…don't cry…don't…' He patted the boy's shoulder. 'Come on now. It's origh'. No harm done.'

The boy shook his head, mumbling something into his hands.

'Whassat now?'

The boy removed his hands. 'My boyfriend dumped me,' he wailed. 'I've been up for literally three days straight.'

'Ah, shit. That's a stinger. Why?'

'I cheated.' The boy's mouth was gluey with strings of saliva. 'I'm a piece of shit.'

'Aw, now, don't say that.'

He sank against Gareth's chest, shuddering with tears. Gareth wrapped an awkward arm around him. 'Get it all out, mate,' he said. And he went on holding him with one arm, using the other to bring the bottle of ruby red liquor to his mouth.

Dawn. Empty bottle of Aftershock. A hazy shaft of light coming in through the gap in the curtains. Tentative birdsong in the trees outside. The boy lay on the bed, on his side, asleep.

Gareth found a bald duvet, yellowed with age, and draped it over him. He patted his head with the flat of his hand.

'Bye,' he whispered.

He crept out of the room and found a plastic beaker full of cider in the hall. There was a fag-end at the bottom. He tossed it on the floor and the liquid splashed his shoes. He stood still for a while, sticking his tongue through the gap in his teeth, his eyes vacant. Then slowly started walking from room to room. People were still up, but most looked at Gareth from bleary bloodshot eyes.

He opened one door. The dark, thick-curtained room was empty of furniture and it smelt like a toilet. Simone, or whatever her real name was, sat on the floor cross-legged in red knickers and a matching, spindly bra, her dress screwed up by her feet. She was skinning up using her fluttering knee as a surface.

Jimmy lay on his back in just his jeans, flies open, a shocking nest of the thickest, blackest pubes spilling out. His skinny white torso was covered in felt-penned doodles. A dead fag-end was stuck to his drooping lower lip. He was asleep.

'Oh, hiya, Mr Moon,' she said, her head rolling round on her shoulders, big grey eyes googly with drink and drugs. 'Listen.' She fixed Gareth in her drunken sights. Blinked slowly. 'I think your mate's shat himself. Be a doll and get him out of yer, will you?'

Not So Manic Now

When Bryan gave the dress back there was cum on it.

It was long, black and vampy, the dress, and it had originally belonged to an ex-girlfriend of mine. I'd let Bryan borrow it for our Halloween shift at Hindley's, a grimy rock club famed for its bad smells. I wore what I usually wore – baggy Hindley's T-shirt over a long-sleeved top, short skirt and fishnets. The dress fit Bryan perfectly. I helped him put on some eyeliner, mascara and lipstick, and stuffed the bra underneath with balled-up toilet paper. When the doors opened at eleven and all the zombies, witches and Goths flurried in like black leaves, Bryan got into character, flicking his hair and giggling while he poured pints of watered-down Carling.

Bryan was camp. But he was not gay.

'Am I woman enough for you now, Lou?' he purred, running his hands silkily over his chest.

I rolled my eyes and poured a pint of snakebite and black for a clearly underage Goth with white face paint clogged in her moustache hairs. 'No One Knows' by Queens of the Stone Age came on. Bryan wrapped his arms around me from behind. 'Can we make sweet lesbian love?'

I felt something hard poke me. 'Bugger off, Bryan!'

'Oops, sorry,' he said, blushing and running away.

No, he was not gay.

At the end of the shift, we drank cans of Fosters in his

flat. He showed me his oil paintings and played The Stone Roses, until I told him I hated The Stone fucking Roses. He kept the dress on.

Around dawn, I curled up on Bryan's bed while he lay next to me, stroking my scabby arms and telling me I was beautiful and that it made him sad when I cut. After a while I fell asleep.

I guess that's when Bryan messed the dress.

I was nineteen when I started considering men. I'd just come out of a relationship with a girl I'd suspected was just playing gay, or confused – I dumped her after I caught her watching *Hollyoaks* while I was going down on her. I thought, Maybe I should give them a proper go? Men, that is.

I went out with Bryan one night. We bought some pills from the Slaughterhouse Inn, swallowed them down with warm lager and came up holding hands in the dark, dewy cemetery across the road. He wouldn't let go of my hand. There was a guy slumped against a gravestone, swaddled in a sleeping bag. Bryan cried, stroking my finger joints with his thumb in slow circles. 'If you care that much, do something about it,' I said. He took off his army surplus coat and gently draped it over the man. 'That cost me forty quid,' he told me.

Back at his flat, Bryan read out some poetry he'd written for me, eyes big, teeth grinding between stanzas. He played me 90s indie music I'd never heard before – Drugstore, Tindersticks, Ride, Mansun. We ended up sat on the floor in our underwear, kissing.

The next morning, we decided to be girlfriend and boyfriend.

*

Bryan was twenty-seven, eight years older than me. He was short for a guy, around five-foot-seven, with a nice toned body. There was an inexplicable dent in his chest, a small hollow, as if someone had poked him too hard as a baby. He sweated a lot and had to take frequent baths. He had a brilliant smile and a massive dick.

We would drink beer in the park with his friends, all twenty-something post-grads who looked at me with suspicion because I was nineteen and possibly a lesbian going through a phase.

Sometimes I would have this feeling when we were doing it. This detached feeling. Like something was wrong. Like when you're near the end of your class-A high and spiky little shocks of come-downy reality start zapping at you. But I would ignore it and it would go away. And I'd remember how my first sex dream, at the age of twelve, had been about David Bowie, and surely that meant something?

Almost every day that summer I would have to run and find a toilet because there was cum dribbling down my leg. I felt like a proper girl.

My best friend Christine thought Bryan was beautiful. Christine was a die-hard Manics fan; she had a dyed black fringe sweeping the forehead, black eyeliner a centimetre thick, wore leopard-print blouses and had 'La Tristesse Durera' tattooed across her chest. She was almost ten years older than me; we'd met at a group for gay self-harmers. She'd been in Whitchurch mental hospital as a teenager ('Same ward Richie went to,' she often boasted, meaning Richie Edwards). The scars slish-slashing her arms looked like skin-coloured slugs. She hadn't cut in a couple of years but she was getting into starving herself. She wanted her ribs to look like ripples in the sand. Or so it said in the sonnet she posted on MySpace.

'Oh, he's lovely,' she said, over the phone, when I told

her I was going out with Bryan. 'He's the only man I would ever consider shagging. Besides Nicky Wire of course.'

'You keep your hands off, you old dyke,' I said, laughing. Because I was supposed to feel threatened by that sort of talk.

We took flowers. We followed the network of white corridors to her ward and there she was on a white bed, a tiny bone-thing. Christine. She smiled weakly. Her meatless limbs were covered in a blonde downy fur and her eyes were too big for her face, her eyelashes seeming longer than usual. She looked like a terrifying doe.

'How are you doing, Chris?' I said.

She just nodded slowly with this air of real dignity. She was hooked up to a drip.

'We bought you some flowers,' said Bryan, holding them out.

'Aw, thanks guys,' she said, taking a raggy breath. 'That's lovely of you. What's goin' on' – breath – 'with you two?'

Me and Bryan looked at each other.

'Nothing really,' I said.

'We got engaged,' said Bryan, flashing his ring.

I wanted to kick him.

'Aw, that's lovely.' – Breath – 'It's beautiful.'

'It's only Elizabeth Duke,' I said, quietly.

A young man came in the room. He was beefy, with scraggly red hair and arms covered in bad tattoos. He fussed over Christine, checking her drip. Me and Bryan looked at each other, swapping small-mouthed humourless smiles. The man leaned in close to Christine. It looked like he was getting something out of her eye.

'This is Mark,' she told us.

Mark nodded and we shook hands. His hand was pleasantly warm.

'I'm her boyfriend,' he said.

'Boyfriend?' I said.

Christine nodded. Mark sat on the edge of the bed and took Christine's bone-knobbled hand.

'He's been looking after me.' – Breath – 'We're in love.'

'Oh,' I said. 'That's really nice.'

Christine looked down at her blanket and smiled like she had a mysterious female secret.

'Do you think they ever have sex?' I asked Bryan, out in the corridor.

'Maybe it's about love, you cynical cow,' he said.

'Yeah, because lust has *nothing* to do with relationships,' I said, grabbing his crotch.

'Oi,' he said. 'You'll give me a semi.'

'Do you think Christine ever gives Mark a semi?'

'Lou!'

We passed through the hospital concourse. We stopped outside and I brought out my tobacco and started rolling.

'I think she's jumping on my bisexual bandwagon,' I said.

'Not everything's about you, darling.'

'It so is.'

'Really, Lou? Has all your empathy flown away?'

'I'm only using humour as a coping mechanism, Bryan. I'm worried about her. She looks horrible.'

Bryan nodded. 'We should try and visit her lots.'

I thought about Christine, her gaunt, fluffy face and spider leg lashes, her queasy and inexplicable love. I didn't want to visit her again. I wanted nothing to do with all that.

There was one a few feet in front of me, sitting cross-legged on a beach towel, reading a novel, another to my right, sunbathing topless, her tits splayed like big white blancmanges, another in a yellow bikini playing Frisbee.

Bryan had taken me to Majorca for my twentieth, joking that if we liked it, maybe we'd come back for our honeymoon. Eliciting a blank-eyed smile from me. We'd spent the morning walking around the Moorish courtyards and galleried arcades of El Torreno, getting burnt. Exotic flowers like butterfly wings spilled from plant pots outside gun shops run by old men who couldn't speak English. There were gun shops everywhere.

A big-hipped woman, also topless, with deep-brown skin except for the startling-white bikini mark. She was swiping sand off the sole of one foot.

I was trying to read. Bryan had given me *The Unbearable Lightness of Being*, saying it was 'a bit hard-going at times, but well worth sticking out,' and I was trying, I was really trying. But there were all these women around. I'd been on the same paragraph for ages. I couldn't stop thinking about women. Could not stop.

Bryan was lying on his stomach, a book open under his chin. 'Shall we go for a swim soon?' I said.

He lifted his glasses and squinted at me, his upper lip pulled up in a gormless snarl. 'I can't,' he whispered.

'Why?'

'I've got a hard-on.'

I sat up and re-arranged my bikini top. 'You've always got a fucking hard-on.' He let his sunglasses drop. They were grubby. His skin was covered in moles, freckles, zits and red sun spots. The sun glinting off his engagement ring was a small white explosion.

We were miles from Magaluf – a deliberate decision – but decided one night to bus it down there, thinking it would

135

be funny. We made our way through the crowd, passing a man kneeling on the pavement with lumpy, brown vomit all over his T-shirt; three men dressed up as nuns; a bunch of young women in furry pink bikinis, bent over laughing. The hot air stunk of jasmine, fag smoke, kebab meat and Jean Paul Gaultier aftershave. There were inflatable cocks everywhere. I held onto Bryan's belt and took everything in.

We came to BCM, a large square building lit up bright, a long white banner draped over its entrance saying, 'MAGALUF'S PREMIER NIGHTCLUB – GET IN!!!' It was packed. We got drinks and stood around looking at people. Some female dancers came out onto the tall podiums. They were toned and thin and within minutes, glossy with sweat. I stared up at them.

'Just going for a piss,' said Bryan, kissing my shoulder.

A small Spanish-looking man with a thick moustache was leaning against a pillar. 'Coke?' he said to me.

'What?'

He pressed a finger against one nostril and acted out doing a line.

'You buying or selling?' I said.

His mouth spread into a wide smile, revealing a row of uneven yellow teeth. 'Ah. You come.' He walked off, beckoning me with his hand. 'Come.'

I followed him. He was short with broad shoulders and a barrel chest – a Danny DeVito physique. He was wearing a clean white vest and grey trousers and had thick black hair combed back.

He led me out of the club, down the steps, passed a few pissed stragglers. 'Where are we going?' I said, and he turned and said something in Spanish, pointing to the end of the street.

'I don't know what you're saying,' I said.

But I continued to follow him.

We came to a car park. It was full of cars but no people and it was dark. 'Ah,' he said, pointing at a silver hatchback. He pulled a key fob out of his pocket, aimed it at the car and I heard the doors unlock, followed by a 'beep beep'. He steered me toward the passenger side and opened the door. 'Come,' he said. His big brown eyes were happy. I thought about Bryan. I got into the car. He came round to the driver's side and got in, still smiling.

It usually takes me a few days to realise I've been indulging in reckless behaviour. I'll drink too much, fuck the wrong sort of people and then I'll have a moment. A conversation with myself. In this hatchback, looking at the man's thick moustache, I was having the moment in real-time. 'Clearly, you want to die,' I told myself. 'You didn't come here for coke, you came here to die.' And again, I thought of Bryan.

The man opened his glove compartment, pulled out a CD and a small paper wrap. 'Coke,' he said, licking his top lip. 'Bueno.' He tapped some out onto the CD (it was Dr Dre), pulled a credit card out of his pocket and started shaping out a line.

'No,' I said. 'I want to buy some. I don't want yours.'

'Eh?'

'I want to buy some,' I said, rubbing my thumb and forefingers together to signalise money. '*Buy* some.'

He flapped his hand at me and went back to setting the line out.

It was a clean car and it smelled nice. There was a meter on the dash. Maybe this was a taxi? I glanced at the open glove compartment. There was a gun inside, a small black gun.

He was smiling again. He lifted the credit card to his mouth and slowly slid his tongue along its powder-coated edge. He handed me the card and signalled for me to look at it. It wasn't a credit card after all – it was some sort of identity card with his picture on it. And there was his name. Jorge Colomar.

'Jorgay Colomar,' I mumbled.

'No,' he said. 'Hor-hay. *Hoor*-hay Colomar.'

'Horhay.'

He looked at the Warhol tattoo on my arm for a while, inspecting it like someone who knows tattoos, running his fingers over it. Then he took out a note from his pocket, rolled it up and slipped it between my fingers.

'Thank you,' I said.

His eyes had gone all soft. He whispered something, gazing at my mouth, then he leaned over and started kissing my neck, his moustache scratching my sunburn. He moved on to my ear and started nibbling it. I could feel his breath in my ear. There was a single greasy fingerprint on the shaft of the gun.

Slowly, very slowly, he moved his hand up my bare thigh and I just held the rolled-up note, frozen. I'm not scared of men usually. I've taunted men in not-very-public places because I have faith that they've been hardwired not to hit women, even if they want to. But there was that gun. Horhay's hand crept under my skirt and edged towards my knickers. His finger poked at the elastic.

I pushed open the door and jumped out and I ran, waiting for the click of a safety catch, my heartbeat thumping in my throat. And soon I was clear of the car park. And soon I was a block away from the car park. And soon I was on a street with people. I stopped to catch my breath.

138

I was still clutching Horhay's identification card.

I decided I would keep it. Next time I wanted to do something stupid I would take it out of my wallet and look at it.

I walked back to BCM and found Bryan. His hair was damp with sweat and stuck to his forehead and he was worried, he'd been looking *everywhere* for me. He grabbed me by my shoulders and looked into my face with a furious intensity and then he started crying. His fingers were digging into my sunburnt skin. I shoved him off me. I shoved him so hard that he fell onto his arse and a bunch of men cheered. He sat on the floor, crying into his hands.

The next day we stayed by the pool all day. Bryan was pretending to sleep on the sun lounger with a towel over his head and his back turned to me. Kids of various nationalities splashed around in the shallow end of the pool and reggae music floated from a second-floor balcony. A couple of obvious-looking lesbians were lying on the grass near the bar, one butch, the other slightly less butch. They weren't attractive but I imagined how they would look fucking, the pair of them white and wobbly and sweating, their fleshy legs plaited together. I looked over at Bryan. One side of his swimming trunks was bunched up the crack of his arse, exposing a blazing-white buttock. I finished my warm beer and opened another.

Around midday a man came out pushing a girl in a wheelchair. The man was thirty-ish with skin the colour of golden syrup and lots of curly body hair and the girl was lame with a tilted, vacant head and wasted legs. The man lifted her out of the wheelchair, cradling her in his arms, and gently made his way down the pool steps into the water. The kids at the shallow end came over and surrounded him.

139

He lowered the girl into the water, still cradling her, and she hung there limply, her eyes unseeing, her long skeletal legs floating. The man was so tender and the children stroked her hair with a gleeful sort of kindness. He let her body swish through the water, setting off lazy, sun-glittered ripples. Two of the older children took the girl off him and together they held her, supporting her slanted head and letting her long black hair fan out mermaid-like. The man looked on, smiling with only a fraction of sadness. This was his reality. The children were so sweet with her. I wasn't used to seeing children so sweet. The girl's eyes gave out nothing, but still they surrounded her, laughing, stroking, stretching out her entropied legs, trying to give her an experience. Trying to give her something.

A week later, me and Bryan held each other, crying along to a Beth Orton CD. Trying to give each other something. Or take something away. Both. I'd told him that his insecurities were ruining everything and he'd let loose a fat teardrop and said, 'I know, but I can't help it, I just love you so much it scares me.' He had every reason to be insecure. This is what happens when you treat humans like guinea pigs, I thought, wiping my tears and snot on his sun-scabbed shoulder. This is what happens when you forget that men have hearts as well as cocks.

That night I drank two bottles of cheap white wine and came to in the bed of a butch forty-eight-year-old with inverted nipples. Horhay Colomar's ID was on the carpet next to my knickers and bra. I must have considered it. I must have pulled it out of my wallet and looked at it, remembering that feeling of danger – too much danger – and self-loathing. Perhaps I was sitting on the edge of the bed and she was behind me, fondling my tits and kissing my back. 'What's that you got there?' she might have asked. 'Nothing,' I would have said, letting it drop to the floor.

I went to visit Christine at the hospital. On my own. Her melancholic skull-like face was surrounded by an over-sized baby-pink woollen hat that made her look, frankly, both ridiculous and creepy. Mark was there, reading a magazine in one of the armchairs. I sat on the edge of the bed and asked Christine how she was doing.

'Not great,' she said.

I stared at my hands.

'They weighed me today.' Breath. 'I'm four stone eleven.'

I thought of the Manic's song. 'Just four pounds to go,' I said.

Her legs were as thin as the crippled girl from the swimming pool. I wanted to grab her by the shoulders and shake her stupid bones.

'I had a coffee yesterday, with milk.' Breath. 'That was a big deal for me.'

'Semi-skimmed,' said Mark, looking up from his magazine.

'How are you and Bryan?' she said.

'Not so good. I don't think I'm bisexual enough. Ya know?'

'Does Bryan know?'

'I think he's getting an idea.'

'Is he OK?'

'He keeps threatening suicide.'

'He shouldn't do that. That's wrong of him.'

'I know.'

Mark had stopped reading his magazine. He was looking at me.

'So you're going to break up –' breath 'with him?' said Christine.

'I'm gonna have to. It's fucking horrible.'

'You have to do what's best for you,' she said, her large doe eyes blinking wisely. 'You have to –' breath 'be kind to yourself.'

I stared at her face with my mouth dropped open. And then I burst into tears.

'Oh, don't be silly. Come here,' she said. I leaned forward and she wrapped her skeleton arms around me and I cried into the cup of her collarbone. Mark came over and rested his warm hand on my shoulder.

God And The Roach

2011

'I don't want anything to do with your dick.' She sipped her drink, permitting her puddle-coloured eyes to rise up to his face. 'I'm not touching it.'

He lifted a clean hand. 'I'm not expecting anything like that.'

'Good.' She leaned forward, her hands laced together. 'We're going to have to establish a safe word. In case I push you too far.'

He glanced around, the light bouncing off his spectacles. 'Really, I don't think you *can* push me too far.'

'Really?' she said, raising a thin blonde eyebrow. 'So if I told you to eat a whole bucket of dog shit? Or I told you to kill someone?'

'Oh, well, I – I wouldn't be able to do *that*.'

'Exactly. The safe word is "pickle".' The waiter brought the espresso and a small stem ginger biscuit. She nodded her thanks and added five cubes of sugar. 'This is no dungeon job. If I want you to just come in, clean my flat, then piss off, you do it.'

A blush spread up his neck. 'That would be – that would be perfect.' He fidgeted around in his seat.

She swallowed her coffee in one and delicately placed the china cup on its saucer. 'We're done.' She stood up, pushing the chair back with her large horse-like thighs. 'You're paying for this meal.' She grabbed her handbag. 'And from now on your name is Roach and mine is God. Good bye, Roach.'

Her flat was on the top floor of a large terraced house. He knew the street because his mother-in-law had lived and died in the care home a few doors down and was now buried in the cemetery over the road. He buzzed up and she let him in. He was dressed in a navy-blue suit that fit his small frame well. Black leather shoes, maroon and silver tie. His wedding band was in his front pocket.

He reached the top of the stairs and she opened the door, wearing a blood-red dressing gown, her voluminous masses of ginger corkscrews tumbling over her shoulders.

'Roach,' she said.

He smiled. 'God.'

Her eyes squeezed up. 'I didn't give you permission to speak. Go back down the stairs and come back up on your hands and knees.'

He nodded, eyes large and child-like behind his swimmy spectacles. He ran down the stairs, reached the bottom, got on his hands and knees and began crawling up. The stair edges dug into his shins. When he got to the middle floor a woman holding a full bin liner opened her door. His head sunk down and he carried on crawling.

He reached the top, panting.

'Cockroaches stay on the floor,' she said.

He washed the dishes, swept and mopped the floor, polished the cupboard doors, cleaned out the oven, the fridge. In his trousers and shirt, the sleeves rolled up, his hairy forearms smudged with brown grease. She stayed in her living room, on the couch. Sometimes she clapped her hands and called out, 'Roach!' in a mean bark and he would come scuttling in,

144

He slotted the vacuum plug into the socket and looked around the bedroom. The walls were painted a purple-maroon and the floor was dark varnished wood, half-covered by a huge Indian rug. There was a Lucien Freud print on one wall, a signed and framed poster of Buffy the Vampire Slayer on the other, though Roach recognised neither artist nor character. He looked in her bookcase. Lots of fantasy and horror and a whole shelf dedicated to books about this vampire-slaying character. A tall pile of Cat Woman comics.

On top there was a framed picture of God with a woman who had to be her mother. The same hair and eyes but leaner, older, with cheekbones and eye-wrinkles. They were hugging. The warmth in God's eyes was jarring. Roach was reminded of the time he took his grandson to Disneyland Paris and they'd caught Donald Duck smoking a cigarette behind Space Mountain, his stuffed duck head under one arm. The sound of a fourth wall falling down with a slam.

The cordless phone on the bedside table let out a robotic trill and he took it to her. She was lying in the bath, the tops of her knees sticking out and her large white breasts floating on top of the bubbles.

Outside he pressed his ear to the door.

'Hey, Mum. I was going to ring you after my bath. What did the doctor say?'

Roach sat on the floor as quietly as he could.

'Hang on a minute, Mum. Roach! You sneaky piece of worthless shit! Get to the kitchen and start cooking my dinner. Now!'

Roach heard the front door close. God traipsed back in looking tired.

'Clean up the nuts,' she said, collapsing onto the sofa. 'Eat them. I hope you have an allergy. Et cetera, et cetera.'

She had just said goodbye to the last party guest. Empty wine glasses and snack bowls covered the coffee table.

Roach, dressed in a butler suit, crawled along the carpet picking nuts up and popping them into his mouth like a squirrel. He was expected home some hours ago. It really was getting rather late.

'Go and make me a sandwich,' she said.

He crawled to the kitchen, hearing the phone go off in the living room. He got some bread from the bread bin and opened the fridge, pulling out margarine and sliced ham. Apparently, God had once been a vegan. He knew this because he had overheard one of her party guests cajoling her about the cheese spread. 'Come back to the dark side, have you?' he'd said to her, smirking. 'Go fuck yourself, Adam,' she replied, good-naturedly, a Boursin smeared cracker in her hand.

God came into the kitchen, phone hanging limply at her side. Her face moon-white.

'I need to go to the hospital. Have you got a car?'

She didn't start to cry until they reached the Gabalfa interchange. Her face fell into her hands and her body started shaking. Roach kept his eyes on the road.

'I'm really scared,' she said.

He said nothing.

'I'm – I'm – I've never been this *scared* before.'

He flicked his indicator and the car filled with calm ticks.

'Why aren't you talking? Why aren't you saying anything?'

He glanced her way, helplessly.

'For fucksake, we're not playing any more, what's wrong with you?'

'OK, OK, sorry,' he said. 'What is it?'

Tears leaked out of her red-rimmed eyes. 'My mum.'

'What happened?'

'I don't know. Heart attack.'

Eyes on the road he leaned over and patted her hand. 'I'm sure it'll be OK.'

He turned into the hospital car park and slotted his silver Audi into the first space. God swung her door open and started running toward the hospital concourse. Roach followed, long black coat fluttering behind him. God went through the main doors and carried on running, past reception, past X-Rays, following signs, and Roach click-clacked behind her in his patent black loafers. They reached the Cardiac Surgery Intensive Care Unit.

'Megan Guinness?' she said to the receptionist, between breaths.

'Are you a relation?' asked the receptionist.

'Daughter.'

'Room 8. Just round the corner. Your father's already in there.'

'*Step*father. Thank you.' God rushed off, scarf trailing behind, her huge pumping buttocks making a frenzy of her long black skirt.

She reappeared some time later. Roach dropped a tatty *National Geographic* on the floor. She came and sat next to him. Her eyes were like candy floss.

'Is there anything you want me to do?' asked Roach.

She fell into him, pulling his arm around her.

'I'm Dawn,' she said. 'What's your name?'

'Jeremy.'

Jeremy stared into her scalp. Things were never going to be the same again. It had all changed.

Pickle, he thought. *Pickle*.

Piss on the Flames

1996

Get home at half five. Put the washing on. Peel the veg.

Holly put some gloves on and grabbed a handful of toilet paper.

Get the chicken ready. Quick hoover.

She bent down and wiped away the diarrhoea. Grabbed the lukewarm flannel from the sink, soaped it up, wiped again.

Quick bath while it all cooks, put the washing in the – oh shoot! Buy washing powder.

She wrung out the flannel in the water, watching as it turned a muddy brown. Imagine I was dying of thirst and someone offered me that? She wrinkled her upper lip. Don't be weird, Holly!

'There we go, Marge, my lovely.'

Maybe a glass of wine, that nice one from Tesco that tastes like Gooseberries. Corrie, Brookside. Could even—

Marge farted. A wet one. Gravy-like poo bubbled out and started dribbling down Marge's thigh.

'Sorry,' said Marge.

'That's OK, da'lin'.' She repeated the whole process. Finally placed a huge incontinence pad into the gusset of the pants, pulled them up, tucked the vest in and pulled the trousers up. Gloves off.

'There we are.'

'Thank you.'

'You're welcome, my treasure.'

She held open the toilet door for Marge, following her out into the hall and down toward the dining room. Marge hunched over her frame, back a question mark, clunky orthopaedic boots scraping the floor Frankenstein-slow.

She stopped and peered round at Holly through bifocals so thick her eyes were the size of goldfish.

'I think I have to go again.'

'Marge. You've just been.'

'Yes, but this time I need to spend a penny.'

Holly smiled. 'OK, da'lin'.'

She'd been at Hillvale (affectionately known as Hellville by staff) for over ten years. Originally it had been a part-time job but her circumstances had changed and now she was averaging a forty-five-hour week. It wasn't like she needed to work all those hours – Dave was bringing in a decent wage from the garage. But it was best to keep busy.

Hillvale had once been a small private psychiatric hospital. Holly remembered passing it on the way to school and imagining all the patients tied up and dribbling, which may or may not have been the case. Things were a lot different now, in psychiatric hospitals and in care homes. Some of the older Hillvale staff remembered back to when a carer could restrain a resident by sitting on them. Holly didn't like to imagine how many ribs had been broken. She was glad things had changed. Still, it was awfully hard sometimes, dealing with the demands of the elderly, especially the ones with Alzheimer's. You couldn't do right for wrong! But Holly felt you just had to get on with it – no sense sitting around moaning when you could be making the best of things.

She dipped the spoon into the soup and brought it up to Enid's lips. 'Come on, love. A bit more.'

Enid smiled. 'Yes.'

'Open up then.'

Enid's mouth opened, revealing a row of smooth pink gums. The spoon went in. She pulled a face. 'I don't like it.'

'Well you did two minutes ago.'

Enid squinted up at her. 'I sat the – I sot the – the price. Can you tell me where it is?'

'Let's try some sandwiches, shall we? Look – salmon. Your favourite.'

Holly heard slow, leisurely footsteps behind her: Cecelia Baker, strolling across the dining room, a sly smile on her lips. One wet fist dripping over her blouse.

'What have you got there, hun?'

Cecelia's smile got slyer. She swung the hand to her hip.

Holly stood up. 'Come on – what've you got there?'

A shake of the head. That smile, lips curling over three craggy teeth the colour of amber resin.

Holly grabbed her wet hand and prised it open. Lying in the centre of the palm was a dead goldfish, squished up, a thread of black faeces hanging out of one end.

'Oh, Cecelia. That's Berty. You've – oh, Ce*celia*.'

Cecelia stared. Cake crumbs stuck to her wiry chin hairs like nit eggs. Her hand clamped back down on the fish corpse and she walked away, smiling placidly.

Holly turned back to Enid who was pouring squash over her sandwiches, a cool, analytical expression on her face.

She laughed, a hand over her mouth. 'Well, Enid. If I didn't laugh, I'd cry.'

'Yes,' said Enid.

*

She brought him a cup of tea and a smile. 'There you are.'

He took a sip and put the mug on his thigh.

They both looked at the TV. An MFI commercial.

'Work OK?' he said.

'Oh, the usual. Understaffed. Evil Audrey was on one – she threw a lamb chop at the cook at lunchtime and then—'

'What's for dinner?'

'Casserole. Chicken.'

He nodded, eyes on the TV. It was that Budweiser one with the frogs.

Holly glanced at the side of her husband's face, his pockmarked cheeks and auburn stubble, the skin on the side of his nose wrinkling up (he loved this advert). It was nice to see him smile. *Brookside* came on. She cuddled up to him, laying her head against his chest. She could feel his heart beating. Just about.

She stayed there for a minute then abruptly moved away.

'I'll go start on dinner.'

He nodded, eyes on the TV.

Connie folded the napkins. Holly sorted the cutlery. Napkin, knife, fork, spoon.

'And the bloody joke,' said Connie, 'is this place isn't even supposed to *have* EMI. It isn't *registered* EMI. It's residential. Yet half the bloody rezzies are nursing or EMI. Does my head in – no, Hol, Arthur doesn't need a knife, he has it liquidised, remember?'

'Ooh, sorry, my mistake,' said Holly, taking the knife away.

'What are you doing?' A small, plump lady stood watching them from the end of the dining room. Black slacks, pink blouse, small, lipless mouth curved like a beak.

Standing there, hands neatly pressed together. Evil Audrey. 'Who are you?' she said, with a gentle West Wales accent.

'I'm Holly, da'lin. I work here.'

The old woman looked her up and down suspiciously, raising her pinky to her mouth and nibbling on it. 'So do I – I've worked here for years.' The pinky came out of her mouth. Went to her eye and scratched at the corner, pulling the baggy skin up and down. 'I might as well make the tea.' Finger went on scratching, pulling the skin down so far Holly could see the pink slimy flesh underneath the eyeball.

'No, we're OK, Aud. Got everything under control. But thank you.'

'Careful, she's been on one all day,' whispered Connie. 'I am a fat bitch and a guttersnipe apparently.'

'Is there anything I can do to help?' said Audrey.

'Not at the moment,' Holly said. She walked up to Audrey, placing a gentle hand on her upper arm. 'Aud, why don't we—'

Audrey slapped Holly's face with a perfect *clap!* 'Don't touch me! Silly bitch.'

Connie was suddenly there, large round body sliding in between the two women. 'Audrey, you don't *hit* people! Holly, you OK, babe?'

Holly nodded, her hand on her cheek. She shouldn't have approached her like that. She *was* a silly bitch.

She went out the garden by the laundry bins and the fag butts and cried noiselessly into her plastic apron. There were voices coming from the tool shed around the corner. Quiet murmurs. She stood listening for a while and soon she recognised them: Hatima, the Indian woman who had started work a few months back and George the handyman, hair and moustache a lovely chestnut brown. Apart from the beer gut, a nicely built man.

Holly peeked around the corner. There they were behind the toolshed window. George had his arms wrapped around Hatima's round hips. Their kiss was a long, slow one. She moved her hand through his hair. Holly stared at the hand. Her bright Indian gold rings flickered under a dusty beam of sunlight. Dazed, Holly looked back at their faces, brown and pink, pressed together, moving from side to side slowly like cement mixing.

She wiped away her tears and smiled broadly. How nice for them. She noticed the knife still in her hand. Oh, what must she look like?

I want to make love, Dave.

Something like that.

Call me old-fashioned but I don't want you to just stick it in me, Dave. Make *love* to me, like you used to.

Maybe it didn't need to be said. Maybe actions would be enough. A soft kiss on the jawline, a hand in his hair. Just a look.

Dave came home with tired, joyless eyes and black grease on his cheekbone. Holly stopped him in the hallway.

'Hello, you,' she said.

He frowned. 'Hmm?'

She smiled up at him. 'I'm just saying. Hello, you.'

'Pissed, Hol?'

'No. Just the one glass.' She rarely had more than just the one glass. He was just jealous because he couldn't drink. 'A dry drunk,' her sister often said, 'is in some ways even worse than a drunk.' And Holly could see the truth in that.

Dave unbuttoned his denim jacket. Holly reached out to touch his cheek. 'Why don't we—'

'I'm having a shower.'

He went up the stairs.

She noticed some fluff on the carpet and picked it up. That dreadful hoover – its only job was to suck things up and it couldn't even do that properly.

Michelle strode past, a rolled-up nappy held out at arm's length. 'Place is a fucking mad house, Hol. I'm run off my feet.'

Holly shook her head, eyes on the medication chart. 'I wish I could help, hun, but I've got to do the drugs.'

'I wish I was doing some drugs, Holly!'

'Oh, Michelle!' What was she like?

Holly dropped an oval tablet into the pill cup. An old man shuffled into the room, bunched hands clawing away at his padded groin. Richard. Poor man. She remembered a time when he used to whistle big band tunes and smile at everyone.

The buzzer went. She frowned, flipping through the blister packs on the rack.

Richard came up behind her and slipped a hand between her legs. 'There we go, Tracy,' he whispered.

She spun around, dislodging the hand. He looked down at her. Bottom lip hanging, dentures clogged with soggy cornflakes.

'Don't do that, Richard. That's – just don't. Now go and sit down, da'lin'.'

He peered at her through his grubby glasses then turned around and hobbled away on feet that swelled out of his slippers like uncooked sausage meat.

She emptied some beige tablets into the pill pot. Warfarin for Enid. For thinning the blood. Got to be careful with Warfarin. Don't want to cut yourself. Stops the blood clotting. Easy way to kill someone. She shook her head. Don't be weird, Holly.

*

'Hello, my little monkey,' she said to Enid. 'I've got some tablets for you.'

Enid was in the armchair, congealed porridge down her pink nightdress. 'Hello.' She pointed at the toilet door. 'What's that?'

'That's the toilet door, da'lin'. Open your mouth for me.'

Enid pointed at the whiteboard. 'What's that?'

'Today's date, lovely.' All the dementia sufferers had whiteboards in their rooms with bright magnet letters for making words. 'Today is Tuesday, da'lin. May the—'

May the third.

She went over to the windows. May the third. Sneaking up on her like that. 'Let's get some light in here, eh?' She opened the long, gold curtains and almost jumped. Standing on the other side of the window, an empty bin liner hanging from his belt, was George. He was mopping sweat from his sunburnt forehead with the back of one big dirty hand. Chest hairs erupted out of his sweat-marked vest.

Holly's fingers tightened around the edge of the curtain.

'That's a footing of the foot,' said Enid.

'Hmm?'

George waved. She waved back, feeling silly. Which was silly.

'Let's get these tablets in you,' she said, spinning back to face Enid with a bright smile.

'Piss on the flames,' said Enid, returning her smile.

Dave. On the bed in his boxers, remote control on one thigh, ashtray on the other.

Holly flopped down next to him. She put her head on his chest. The News was on. She wriggled around, getting in closer. Dave smoked and watched the TV. Teenage boy

157

stabbed in London. Three o'clock in the afternoon outside a Post Office.

She tutted. Mindlessly ran her hand over the bobbled surface of Dave's jersey boxers. 'How can people *do* that?' she said.

Dave moved the ashtray from his leg and put it on the bedside table. He lifted Holly's chin and kissed her on the lips. She kissed back softly and only when he put his tongue in her mouth did she grab his hair, his face. He pulled off her T-shirt, flipped her over, kissed her back for a while. There was a pause. She heard him spit once, then twice, and suddenly he was slamming away and breathing loudly through his nose. John Major was talking about a referendum. Dave wrapped his arm around her and rubbed her clitoris with a dry hand and she stared at the clock radio on the bedside table and there was the date blinking underneath the time. May the third.

The room was dark except for a slice of moonlight coming in through a gap in the curtain.

'Dave. You awake?'

'Hmm.'

'Do you know what tomorrow is?'

'No.' He rubbed his jaw and yawned. 'What's tomorrow, Hol?'

'May the fourth. The anniversary.'

'Oh.' He went stiff.

She stroked the coarse hairs on his forearm. 'Why don't we talk about it? Hmm? It might be – I don't know, it might be good to *talk* about it.'

He didn't answer.

'Dave?'

He jerked his arm away from her and jumped out of bed.

'Dave, don't—'

'Leave me alone, Hol.' And he left the room and didn't come back.

Marge: buzzing for the toilet every ten minutes, and when you took her she either didn't need to go after all or had already peed herself. Cecelia: wandering into rooms and taking things – photos, remote controls, asthma pumps. Richard: shouting abuse at the wooden banister outside his bedroom. Arthur: defecating all over the carpet and slipping in it.

'Holly, do me a favour,' said Connie, rushing past with a pile of dirty clothes, her bum and thighs jiggling. 'Will you have a go at doing Evil Audrey? She's taken against me tonight.'

'Oh, what's she done?'

'Called me a nig-nog.'

'Oh, Connie! That's awful.'

Connie kicked open the laundry room door and threw the clothes in. 'I'm not paid enough for racial abuse, know what I mean?'

'I know, da'lin,' said Holly. 'I know.'

The buzzer went off. Holly jumped and put a hand on her heart. 'That awful noise!'

'Bloody tell me about it. It's like Japanese water torture.' Connie went over to the grid on the wall. 'It's Joyce.' She pressed a button and the buzzing stopped. 'I'll get it.'

'No, no,' said Holly. 'You put the kettle on and I'll get it.'

She took the lift up to the top floor. Joyce was a tall thing with balding hair. She was sat on the edge of her bed pulling a baby pink bed sock onto one foot. She looked up at Holly and held out the other sock.

'Put this on.'

159

'Pardon?'

'Put this on for me, will you?'

'But Joyce, if you can do it for yourself then you shouldn't be asking me.'

Joyce stared at her.

'I mean, this is a residential home, da'lin', and we're supposed to encourage inde*pen*dence.'

'Just put it on.'

Holly got on her knees and slid the sock onto Joyce's crooked claw of a foot. 'There we go,' she said, smiling.

'And close my curtains.'

Holly closed her curtains.

'I don't want cocoa tonight.' Joyce sniffed back some snot. 'I want Horlicks.'

'OK, no problem.'

'Oh, and shut the bathroom door.'

Holly shut the door. 'There we go.' Smiled again. Waiting.

Joyce said nothing.

Nothing.

Holly walked out.

Never mind. Never mind.

She went downstairs, stopped outside a room, rapped the door gently and walked in. Evil Audrey sat in her armchair by the window.

'Who are you?' she asked.

'I'm—'

'Don't you know you're supposed to knock a door before entering?'

'I did.'

'You did not.' Audrey stood up, hands curled up in front of her chest like a rodent. 'What d'you want?'

'Actually, maybe I'll come back later.' No sense poking

the hornet's nest – best to wait until she'd had her eight o'clock calmer. She saw an empty cup and saucer on the bedside table and picked them up.

'What are you doing? Those are mine.' Audrey snatched the cup. 'Get out.' She shoved Holly hard, getting her in the left breast. 'Get out of my house!'

Holly ran out of the room clutching the saucer over her hurt breast, and almost bumped into Cecelia, who was clutching a balled-up pad – soiled by the look of it. There were smudges of dark brown on Cecelia's hands.

'Christ.' Holly rolled her eyes. 'Where d'you get that from? Have you been in the bins again?'

Cecelia stared at her.

And then the buzzer went again.

Dear Lord in heaven.

Holly took hold of the nappy. 'Give it here, Cecelia.'

'No.' Those blank eyes. Nothing.

'Cecelia! Give it to me now!' She yanked it out of Cecelia's strong grip. A small splatter landed on Holly's forearm. 'Now come with me. Let me clean you up.'

'No.'

Holly squeezed her eyes shut. Forced a smile.

'Please come with me, Cecelia. You've got poo on you. Please.'

Cecelia's mouth curved into a smile, her big rotten teeth pushing against the crusty lips. 'No.'

'Fine! Walk around covered in someone else's shit then!' She stormed away, jaw tight, headed toward the nearest alarm grid, pad still in one hand. 'I shouldn't have said that,' she thought. 'I should have said poo.' She looked at the flashing LED display. Room 7. Room 7. Marge.

She made her way to Marge's room, went in and turned off the buzzer.

The buzzer went off again.

'Oh flippin' hell!' Someone else. Always someone else.

She passed by a white board: 'HELLO MARGE. TODAY IS WEDNESDAY 4TH OF MAY 1996.' She stood, one hand on her hip, the other clutching the soiled pad. 'What is it?'

Marge looked up at her. 'I need to use the toilet.'

'What? You've just been ten minutes ago.'

'Pardon?'

'I said you just *used* the toilet ten minutes ago.'

Marge blinked slowly. 'Did I?'

'Yes.'

Marge considered this, brow crinkled. Then her eyes drifted back up to Holly. 'Well, I need to go again.'

And that was it. That was *it*.

Holly opened up the soiled nappy and pressed it into Marge's face. She let it drop. Granulated brown shit the consistency of Ready Brek was daubed on Marge's cheeks and chin, a moist chunk dripping off the end of her nose, her glasses thick with it.

She ran out of the room and started running. It was so *hot* in this building! The buzzer went on. She ran past the storeroom and the dusty artificial flowers and the watercolours of beaches in cheap frames. It felt like her eyes were pulsing inside her head. She went into Audrey's room. Without knocking. The woman – the *bitch* – was sat on the edge of her bed, hands laced together over her pot belly. 'Oh there you are,' she said, smiling. 'I thought you'd never come. Did you speak to my mother after?'

'Your mother is dead. And your father. *And* your husband. And you know what? You'll be dead soon and no one will fucking care!'

Audrey stared at her.

162

Holly left the room.

She swayed where she stood, breathing heavily. The buzzer went on. Why wouldn't it stop? She headed toward the lift and pressed the button. Joyce, she thought.

Didn't even say thank you, she thought.

'Didn't even say fucking thank you,' she said aloud.

She was going to give her a piece of her mind. Horrible, spoiled woman, treating the carers like slaves, like stupid slaves. Spoiled rich bitch, thought she was better than everyone just because she married a surgeon and lived in Pontcanna all her life.

Why was *she* allowed to live till eighty-nine?

The lift rose slowly. The buzzer was quiet in here. She stood with her hands limp at her side. Fucking Joyce, she thought. Needs slapping, she does. She got out and passed Una's room, Arthur's room. A good hard slap. She passed Enid's room and paused, looking in. Enid was in bed lying on her back, the duvet covering her up to the hips, staring at the ceiling.

"HeLLo Mrs enid Moon," said the whiteboard. "T0day is Wednesday May 4th + it sunny out." The bright letters splashed across the board like regurgitated rainbow.

Holly climbed onto the bed and huddled up to Enid's warm, fat body. She laid her head on Enid's shoulder and started crying.

'Hello,' said Enid.

The buzzer stopped.

'There it is. A cross – a cr – crystal,' said Enid.

Holly nodded, her face a shiny grimace. She noticed a small splatter of poo on her forearm. From that pad. Who had it belonged to?

She looked up into Enid's face. 'I've done a dreadful thing.'

'Yes,' said Enid.

The Birdmoth

2008

Deena's cast, wrapped in a green recycling bag, was propped up awkwardly on the lip of the tub and kept threatening to slip into the water. She drank some beer and rested its chill base against the bony ridge between her sloping breasts. She could hear her dad mowing the lawn outside. The loud chug-a-chug of him re-starting it every five minutes, and in between, the monotonous *vroooom*, rising and falling, rising and falling.

This was her new thing, drinking in the bath. If the water was hot enough, two bottles of Corona felt more like four. She'd sip them slowly, listening to a podcast about serial killers or conspiracy theories, and afterwards, would clumsily manoeuvre herself out of the tub feeling relaxed, weak and not particularly interested in the remaining beer bottles in the fridge. Well, a little interested. But not enough to make that journey down the stairs to the kitchen (she had to clamber down on her bum). This was the difference between her and Dennis – whereas she did not *want* to stop after just one drink, he had been *unable* to. And that was why he'd ended up dead at the bottom of a flight of stairs with a broken neck and a screaming mother.

A blue-white butterfly flew out from behind the shampoo bottles on the shelf and fluttered over the bath, disturbing the rising steam. It landed on her cast. She twitched her leg and it flew to the window, coming to rest on the glass, its wings spread out. Wasn't symmetry directly related to beauty? She'd read an article about that once. There was a scientific formula for beauty, something about proportion and measurements and Marilyn Monroe's hairline. Mixed-race people were supposed to have the most symmetrical faces. God, the amount of times her and Dennis had taken an E or some M-cat and spent the night planning their future children. 'I want a brown baby,' he'd say, imitating Waynetta Slob from the *Harry Enfield Show*. 'Ma very own turkey baster braaan baybee.'

Actually, she could remember once having a variation of this conversation with him in this very bath. Her parents had gone away for a fortnight, visiting family in Pakistan, and he'd pretty much stayed over the whole time. The house ended up foul, like a squat – bins filled with vomit, ashtrays spilled on the beds, piss on the buttercream couch. One of the days they both chipped in for some MDMA and started doing lines off the dining room table. They ran a bath and got in, she at the tap end, he at the other. He had a chubby penis with a big chrome barbell through the head. They slumped with gurning faces, knee to knee, listening to The Shangri-Las and talking about their future turkey baster brown-babies. Reznor for a boy, Jezebel for a girl.

The day before her parents were due home, he'd pissed off back to his mum's, leaving her to deal with the disgusting mess. The dickhead. He could be such a dickhead.

Something dark fluttered in her line of vision and she jerked upright, causing the water around her hips to make a suction-slurp. A moth. One of those thick, hairy moths with bodies the size of pear drops. Birdmoths. That's what she called them. It plinked against the wall tiles and darted near her face, stopping suddenly on the rim of the bathtub.

Little eyeballs like caviar. She grabbed a shampoo bottle and brought it down on the moth's body and there was a firm, springy sensation. She lifted the bottle and it stuck to the bath edge, its legs and antenna twitching. She shuddered. Horrible things. She lay back, the water lapping against her stomach.

What did that say about her? That a butterfly could fly in and land on her leg and she'd marvel at its delightful symmetry, but a moth, a dirty brown moth had to be murdered *immediately*. What did that suggest? Kill the ugly things and let the pretty ones live? Was she that kind of person? Maybe it was internalised racism? Dennis was always talking about internalised homophobia – he likened it to eating poison. She drained her beer, burped. No. It was just because moths were awful. They flew right in your face. Did not respect boundaries.

She tilted her empty bottle toward the moth. 'Sorry, mate. That wasn't very nice of me.'

Normally she had a wedge of lime squeezed into the neck of the bottle, but her mum had used up all the limes making pickle this morning. She'd stared into the fridge, her mouth stiffening with resentment, ready to start cursing, but then she looked at her mother – she was sat at the kitchen table smoking a fag while doing homework for her NVQ level five, her glasses slipping down her nose. Almost more like a grandma than a mum. 'They weren't even my limes to begin with,' she'd thought. 'What's my fucking problem?'

'Grief is like an impacted shit that has to come out eventually,' her father had told her at the hospital bedside. He had lost a brother when he was young, before marriage and children, and just like with her and Dennis, they'd been on bad terms at the time. 'Very painful,' he said, thumping his breast with his fist. 'I had pretend conversations inside my head for a long time, all the things I should have said to him, you know? But you cannot argue with a dead man.' He'd brought grapes and he ate them himself, handfuls at a time, getting clear juice caught in his moustache. 'These arguments were really with myself,' he said. 'A way of dealing with guilt. But there's nothing we can do about guilt. It's a bitch.'

'Cheers for that exemplary nugget of fucking wisdom, Pa, I feel so much better now.'

That's what she'd been about to say.

The skin under her cast was itching and she was overdue her pain meds. But what if she said it and then he left and, on the way home, he got run over or something? And she had to look down at his stitched-together face in a silk-lined casket with those last words echoing: *Cheers for that exemplary nugget of fucking wisdom, Pa, I feel so much better now.*

Her last words to Dennis? She couldn't even remember. Only the anger and the bilious desire to cut with words.

'Deena!' Her mother's voice coming from the other side of the door in a harsh whisper. 'Deena! I need you to come out!'

She rolled her eyes. 'I'm in the bath! Use the downstairs loo.'

Again, the harsh whisper: 'We are having a situation. Please, come down.'

'Do you know how long it'll take me to get out of the bath and get dressed?'

'What?'

'I said, "Do you know how long it'll take me to get out of the fucking bath and get dressed? With a broken leg?"'

'Deena! Just come downstairs now, please! Family emergency.'

Deena leaned forward to pull out the plug, her stomach fat multiplying into three unsmiling rolls.

She slid down the last few steps, took a hold of the banister and pulled herself to her feet. The towel wrapped around her head started to tilt and she quickly adjusted it. She wedged her crutches under her armpit and turned around to see her mother's fretful face right in front of her own.

'Oh my God,' said Deena, pressing a hand against her heart, 'you should wear a fucking bell.'

'Your language!' her mother said. She was smoking a cigarette and her hand was shaking. 'It is unnecessary.' She started for the living room. 'Come and look,' she said in whispered, excited Urdu, turning to glance at Deena to see if she was following. There was a wildness in her eyes.

Her father was just outside the living room door, waiting for them. He was rubbing his fingers together, thumbs against first two forefingers, and upon seeing them, his hands relaxed and his face sagged. He had specks of mowed grass all up his T-shirt. Deena stopped in the doorway. There was going to be a dead or dying animal on the living room rug. What else? Dad'd been busy mowing, in the zone, and then suddenly the lawnmower goes over something, causing it to buck in his hands and blood to spray out alongside the grass clippings, and he stops and there's next door's cat, or that beadle, beagle – whatever the fuck it is – from across the road, or the alky's fat pigdog from number nine or Lou and Polly's yappy little shih-tzu. There it is, all mangled. And so he gently lifts it in his arms and brings it inside the house and now it's slowly dying, its leg twitching like that birdmoth, and neither of them know what to do about it, and she'll have to be the one to put it out of its misery, bashing its head in with the end of her crutch. Because that's what humans do, she thought – they see pain and suffering in animals and nobly put a stop to it, unless it's happening to another human, in which case, fuck 'em.

'Come and look!' whispered her mum, tugging her dressing gown sleeve.

At first she saw nothing. Because she was looking for blood. She followed her mother's gaze: the settee. Her mouth dropped open and a huffy chest-laugh almost came out, halting at her throat.

The homeless man. The local homeless man. Monsterberry Crush. Asleep on the couch.

She wheeled around to face her mother and father. 'What the fuck?'

Her mother slapped her on the arm and brought a finger to her lips. 'Shhh!'

Wedging the crutches tight in her armpits, she spread her hands incredulously. 'What the *actual* fuck?' she whispered.

'He's been sleeping there for fifteen minutes,' her dad whispered. He came up to them both and took the cigarette out of his wife's hands. He took a long drag, his expression pained, like a man with indigestion. He hadn't smoked in years. 'I'm mowing the lawn and I stop for a break.' Another pained drag, his mouth drawing down at the sides, making him look, with his big moustache, like a Mexican, like a fat, balding Cheech Marin. 'I come in for a drink and he's there, sleeping.' He turned to his wife and handed her the cigarette back. 'He came in when I was mowing, he must have come from the back lane and gone right past me and in through the back door, and I didn't even notice. Why would a man do that?'

'It's the homeless guy from the allotments,' said Deena. Monsterberry Crush.

'We know,' said her father. 'The local pisshead. Here on our couch. Such an honour.'

'Always he's walking around drunk,' said her mother. 'Sometimes I buy him sandwiches. You remember, he was with Ava when she broke out? You remember me telling you? He's very friendly but he is stinking of piss all the time.' She took a long drag of the cigarette, her hands still shaking. 'We haven't finished paying off the sofa. It was very expensive.' This last bit in Urdu.

It was the same couch Dennis had pissed on. Deena had wiped at the dried-in pee with a wet soapy towel hours before her parents were due back from the airport. Then she sprayed it with Febreeze and flipped it over. How strange. A dead man's piss, still infused in the foam. All the bits of himself he left behind.

Monsterberry Crush was on his side with his back to the cushions, curled up a little. He had his shoes on and a stained old army coat. His mouth was open and he was drooling onto the buttercream fabric. She'd chatted with him once in the lanes behind Tamerlane Road. He'd been blind drunk and annoying – just speaking words at her, a broken satellite dish stuck on broadcast, receiving nothing. 'Give him my number next time you see him,' Dennis had said to her, after. 'I'll give him the best blowjob of his life, no questions asked.' His mouth turned up at one side to tell her he was joking. But it was never really a joke. Monsterberry Crush was straight and Dennis liked to suck straight dick.

She turned to her parents. 'Why don't we just wake him up?'

The idea seemed to fill them with horror. Her father raised his hands as if to say, No, don't shoot!

She raised a crutch and hovered it over his head. 'Shall I put him out of his misery?'

Her father rushed forward and snatched the crutch out of her hand. He led her back to the centre of the room.

'I was joking!'

'Shhhh!' said both parents, their fingers to their lips, eyes stretched open.

She stared at their desperate faces, her eyes zipping back and forth from one to the other. And then – she couldn't help it – her body was suddenly racked with huge gulping laughter.

Her parent's eyes stretched even wider, their hands flying to their mouths, as if she'd just said something taboo. And then *they* were laughing, both of them, with that same helpless urgency, and all three stood in a triangle, laughter coming up in waves, their hands on their thighs or their breasts – helpless, gulping, delirious laugher, the best kind of laughter.

Monsterberry Crush jerked upright, half his face wrinkled from the cushion, spit webbing his beard. He took a great dignified breath in through his nose, his head tilting back, and then he was on his feet and walking to the door, blinking rapidly. As he stumbled past, Deena's mother slapped his bum. Her father doubled over, smacking his hand against the coffee table and whooping. Monsterberry Crush turned at the living room door, seemed to think about saying something, and then left.

'Oh my fucking God!' roared Deena, in between breaths.

Her mother, large eyes dancing, grabbed her by the arm. 'Why are you always attracting the alcoholics, Deena?'

Monsterberry Crush

May 4th, 2009

The hot liquid splashed down on Dave's face, pooling in the dip between nose and cheek. He thought for a moment that it might be rain – he often got rained on. He shielded his face with his forearm and pushed himself up onto his elbow. Piss. A small, pale-mauve cock poking out of a nest of black pubes was dangled over his head.

'Knock it off,' he said croakily.

The boy or man laughed. Some tosser on his way home after an all-nighter, full of booze and testosterone and failure, trying to make himself feel better about his various inadequacies. The piss slowed to a trickle. Dave felt a hot droplet hit his earhole.

More laughter. Footsteps retreating.

Fucking cheap shot. He pushed himself fully upright and wiped his face off with his jumper. He looked around himself. It was light and bright, the skies filled with tinkling bird song. He appeared to be in the lane behind Tamerlane Road; there was the allotment fence in front of him, thick brambles poking through the crosslinks. To his right was a tall slate-blue garage door covered in senseless graffiti and above him a small corrugated roof jutting out a few inches – he'd at least found some semblance of shelter last night before passing out. Progress. There were two flagons next to his makeshift pillow (a bundled-up pair of jogging bottoms), one empty, the other half-so. He unscrewed the lid and drank deeply. The sky was light blue and clear though he could see dark clouds rolling in from the east. They'd be here by mid-morning at the latest, he judged, and they'd bring grey skies, buckets of rain and a general sense of gloom. Which was just as well.

She had a bin liner to sit on and a large umbrella to hold, but fortunately, the rain had died down to a ticklish spray. The grass was wet regardless, so she took the bin liner and ripped the seam and laid it out flat on the ground directly in front of the headstone. The ground felt cold and squishy under the plastic. She hadn't come here expecting comfort. All the same, maybe she'd bring a fold-up stool next time. She delved in her bag and brought out a tube of sour cream Pringles and a packet of Jaffa Cakes – his favourite. He used to eat a packet of both each night. She'd always suspected that he smoked marijuana up in his room and these snacks were for the 'munchies' as they were called, but he'd always claimed he was just drunk-hungry. It had taken a visiting friend to point out the smell coming from upstairs. 'That's skunk, that is,' the friend had said, crinkling his nose. How embarrassed she'd been! She'd ransacked his room later that night as he lay passed out on his bed and found the stuff in his tobacco tin. 'Your father'd roll in his grave, ya silly wee dobber,' she'd told him the next morning, holding the cannabis pinched between her finger and thumb in front of his bleary hung-over face. 'How dare you bring drugs into my house! How dare you!'

He'd smiled at her pronunciation of house. 'Oh, come on, it's just a bit of weed, Mum,' he'd said, licking his Rizla and rolling his cigarette expertly despite his shaking hands. 'It's not like I'm bringing crystal meth into your *hoose*.'

She took the lid off the Pringles, peeled back the foil and

took out a crisp. 'I've brought us some munchies, Dennis,' she said, smiling. 'Oh, I almost forgot…' she dipped her hand into in her bag and brought out a small chocolate sponge cake. She'd bought it the day before on her lunch break, deliberating longer than was necessary over finding the right one. She'd gone to the fancy bakery in the arcade and almost ordered a bespoke cake with black icing and sugar skulls before realising she was being foolish (sixty pounds for a dead man's cake!) and stopping off at Sainsbury for a regular sponge. People can get quite silly about the dead, she'd decided.

She went back into her bag, took out a packet of birthday candles and stuck a few in the cake. 'I'm not singing the song,' she said, lighting the candles. 'I'd feel like a tool. That's the right expression, isn't it?' She held up the cake. 'Happy birthday, darling.' And she blew out the little fires, six where there should have been twenty-eight – and counting.

No. There was only so much she could tolerate. She stood up and stared down at the man. He was four graves over, sat with his back against a headstone. She recognised him – she often saw him wandering around the area. Homeless, certainly. He'd been singing at the top of his voice this past hour. He was quite obviously pissed.

'Excuse me,' she said and he looked up, his mouth slack. She had one hand on her hip and her expression was suitably scolding. 'I'm trying to mourn my dead in peace,' she said.

'Why?' he said.

And the question stalled her. Why indeed? Is it what Dennis would have wanted? Peace, quiet, sombre dignity? All the same. Who was this soss-pot to dictate the manner in which she celebrated her dead son's birthday? And fuck him for making her feel like some sort of bereavement spoilsport.

'Because,' she said, 'this is a cemetery, not a pub.'

He seemed to consider this. He had an auburn beard with some grey patches. The skin on his cheekbones was acne-scarred and the tips of his fingernails were black. He wore a big army surplus coat. 'Fair enough,' he said. 'I have been very inconsiderate.' He suppressed a small burp, his eyes glazing. 'I will endeavour to keep it down. My apologies.'

Sighing, she sat back down. The man didn't sing again. She glanced over now and again – he drank from his cider bottle and smoked roll-ups, his back slumped against the gravestone. His dead wife? Mother or father? Child? An old friend? Maybe he was just here because it was somewhere he could go without being moved on by police officers and this headstone was as good as any.

She knew what Dennis would say: why do you care? Do you fancy him or something?

Fancy!

He could always make her laugh, Dennis. Cry too, yes. Most of the time she didn't know whether to hug him or slap him.

She noticed that the drunken man was gone. No, not gone. He was stood a few yards over, his back to her, pissing up against a birch tree.

'Oh, for goodness sake,' she said. What a horrible, horrible man. Well, that was the day spoiled. She grabbed the Pringles and Jaffa Cakes and threw them back into her bag. 'He's worse than you,' she said to the headstone beneath her nose. 'No one could spoil a day quite like you.' She smiled, despite her fury. It was all very fitting actually.

Dennis was always getting drunk and pissing in places he shouldn't.

She scrunched up the damp bin liner and stuffed it into her bag. 'Goodbye darling boy,' she said. She got down on her knees and stroked the stone with a tender hand, as if adjusting a newborn's bonnet, and tidied up the fresh flowers.

The man was still pissing when she walked past. 'Thank you very bloody much!' she said. He turned and the sudden movement caused him to lose his balance. He spun around, arms propelling. Pam caught a glimpse of a fat-headed penis flopping about, the urine still spraying out of it. She brought a hand to the side of her face, blocking her vision like a horse's blinker.

'Oh, I'm sorry,' she heard him call out, 'I'm so sorry for relieving my bladder in a place reserved for rotting corpses! Oh, the injury I have done to the rotting corpses!'

'Go and fuck yourself!' she called back.

May 4th, 2010

'Oh, for God's sake,' the woman muttered as she walked past him. He aimed a frown at her back. Who was she? And why was she so displeased with him? Mind you, some people didn't need a reason. The woman stopped at a small headstone a few plots over and his memory was jogged. That lady from last year! He took a mouthful of cider. Now what had he done to upset her? There were a handful of likely possibilities: he'd used blue language; he'd sung too loudly; he'd come on to her; he'd fallen asleep and pissed his pants. Course, it was also possible that he'd done fuck all and she was just an uptight bitch. A teetotal, curtain-twitching, 'not in my backyard' sort of Tory twat. 'If you give them money they just spend it on drugs and alcohol'. One of those cunts. As if buying alcohol wasn't a logical response to losing everything worth living for.

He watched her unfold a camping chair and take some things out of her bag. Who was he kidding? He'd probably done something terrible. Spoiled her day with his foolishness.

He approached the woman. She was sat in her chair with a packet of Jaffa Cakes and some Pringles on her lap. She sat very neatly, like a lady.

'Afternoon,' he said, smiling, and she rolled her eyes.

'Please leave me alone,' she said. Soft Scottish accent.

He held up his hands, palms out. 'I will, I will. I came over to apologise for whatever I did exactly three hundred and sixty-five days ago.'

'You don't remember?'

'I seldom remember, Ma'am. I find it an advantageous by-product of alcohol abuse.'

'You were…well, you were behaving like an obnoxious drunk to be honest.'

'I *am* an obnoxious drunk. How else should I behave?'

'You could start with no public pissing.'

'I think I can manage that.'

'And don't sing too loudly.'

'Deal.' He smiled. 'Having yourself a picnic?'

She looked down at the food on her lap as if surprised to find it there. 'Aye, a wee picnic.' She had a Maggie Smith vibe, he thought. The accent, the big eyes. Only her teeth were in a worst state than Dame Maggie's and she had a pot belly.

'It's his birthday,' she said. 'Was, I mean. These were his favourite snacks.'

He squinted his eyes and read the words on the stone,

doing some rough arithmetic. Her son. Or toyboy lover. Probably her son.

'Celebrating the old death day, me,' he said, jabbing a thumb over at his previous spot. He pulled a dubbie out of his pocket and lit it. 'Nice idea though, with the food. Course, if it was me, I'd have to be bringing jelly and ice cream.' He smiled sadly. 'Milky bars and sherbet dib dabs and all that shite.' She looked up at him with kind concern. He could use that, if he had a mind to. Women were suckers for grieving fathers, as the last twenty years had proved to him. *Well no wonder he's drunk and unclean – now that I understand his pain I shall endeavour to try to fix it by sitting on his dick.* He got his eyes to twinkling and tipped his flagon at the gravestone, saying, 'Happy birthday, fella.'

He stumbled back to his plot and, true to his word, did not sing loudly nor piss publicly. He could still remember how to be a gentleman.

How had he eaten this stuff *every* night? The Pringles alone were bad enough but the Jaffa Cakes on top, well, it was all junk. No goodness to them. But Dennis had never been interested in what was good for him. His boyfriends for example – manipulative control freaks, each and every one of them. What could possibly have induced him to fall for these creeps? It's not like he'd been raised in a loveless house. She'd accepted his sexuality, as had his father, eventually anyway. And it was such a hard thing for a man to get to grips with. You get these images in your head – your boy, your little boy who you sent off to nursery carrying his little Roland the Rat lunchbox, whose knees you kissed when he fell over, your little sweet boy, and there he is twenty years later, a grown man taking a dick up the – well, it was hard for any parent, but especially a man like Colin. He'd expected a normal boy

– now that wasn't a very nice way to put it – he'd expected a *typical* boy. He'd dreamed of teaching him football. Fat chance! Still, Colin had loved him all the same.

'You all right there?'

It was the homeless man.

She swiped a tear away with her finger and nodded, tight-smiling.

'Doesn't get any easier, does it?'

She shook her head, lips sucked in.

He came down next to her on one knee and patted her shoulder. His face was compassionate and kind but his head was swaying with the drink and he smelled bad and she was worried he'd try and kiss her. Which would be disgusting. Disgusting.

'I'm going to cheer you up,' he said, rummaging through his large pockets. 'I've got just the thing.' He fell back onto his arse, his arms and legs going up in the air. 'Oops. Look at me, falling over already.' He righted himself and brought out a battered book with a ruined spine. 'I'm going to read you a poem.' He licked a finger and flicked some pages. 'It's the best poem in the world apparently.' He glanced up at her. 'Ready? Are you ready for the best poem in the world?'

She nodded, almost bemused.

'"The Trouble with Spain", by Charles Bukowski. Here goes. "I got in the shower and burnt my balls last Wednesday…"'

May 4th, 2011

His eyes cracked open. The lane again. Rain again.

Bollocks to it all.

He propped himself up and was surprised to find that lying across his body from the chest down was a thick duvet and, on top of that, a sheet of tarpaulin. He groped under the layers – dry. He touched his head. Wet. Well, that wasn't so bad. He sniffed the duvet. It smelled like old ladies – lavender, biscuits. The way his mother's house used to smell.

He was startled by a loud mechanical clanging and screeching. The garage door he was lying next to was being cranked up.

'Fuck me,' he said, edging away from the doors. Someone on the way to work probably, wanting to get their car out.

But it was a small old woman. The cranky Irish nutjob who fed the stray cats and always tried to hit him with her walking stick.

He grinned and doffed an imaginary cap. 'Top of da mornin' to ya.'

She fixed him with a scowl. 'Don't you be givin' me any lip, ya workshy eejit,' she said, shuffling forward, her walking stick raised.

'Round two, ding ding,' he said, his arm up to ward off her blows.

She edged closer, crouched down, her stick still high, and quickly snatched the tarpaulin away.

'What the fuck, woman?'

'Mind your mouth!' she screamed. And then she swiped the duvet away.

'You've gone too far now,' he said, pointing his finger at her nose. 'That was keeping me dry.'

She made a throaty noise of disgust. 'Geddaway widja, ya poor excuse for a man!' She hit him over the head with her stick. He clutched his scalp and she struck again, rapping his knuckles. He tried to grab the stick but she was too quick – she got him on the shoulder this time. 'Get off my prauperty. Take your bottles o' piss widja.'

He clambered to his feet. 'It's cider!'

'Same ting.' She did a shooing gesture. 'Off widja, go on now.'

He grabbed his flagon – mercifully still close to full – and, standing tall, looked down at her, all humour gone. He could destroy her. He wanted her to know that. 'You, woman, are a cruel human being devoid of any decency and compassion. You should be ashamed of yourself.'

She raised her sparse white eyebrows sardonically. 'Is dat so? Cruel, am I?' She bundled up the duvet and tarp and dragged them into her garage. 'Next time I'll let you sleep in da pouring-down rain, you ingrate.' She pressed a button on the wall and the door began its loud clanking descent.

He stared at the tiny woman through the shrinking gap.

'I've always said, the Irish are the kindest people in the world,' he shouted. 'No word of a lie, I've always said that.'

She did another shooing gesture.

'You are a queen among women,' he shouted.

Only her legs were left. She had red swollen ankles spilling out of her slippers.

'May your days be bright and your nights restful,' he shouted, and then the door was down.

She popped the cork out and the Prosecco foamed up, dribbling down her wrist and soaking her cardigan sleeve.

'Nice technique,' he said, waggling his eyebrows.

'Oh, be quiet.' She quickly aimed the fizz into a black resin goblet decorated with small skulls – Dennis' favourite drinking vessel. 'You've promised me you're going to behave yourself today.'

'And I will,' he said. 'But you simply must allow me the occasional innuendo or I fear my soul shall shrivel up and die.'

'Like your liver?' she said, raising an arch eyebrow.

He winced as if wounded, whistling in air through pursed lips. 'Below the belt, woman.'

'Would you like a glass? I've got a spare cup with me.'

'Oh no, but thanks. I don't mix my drinks. Even a silly wee pish-head like me has rules to live by.' She smiled at this last bit; it was a good impression.

The day was fine, clear and almost warm. The grass was wet from the night's rain but the gravestones and gravel paths were dry. Dave was wearing a leather jacket instead of his usual army coat. Pam wondered where he kept his clothes. She knew he didn't sleep rough every night because he'd mentioned hostels and sofas last time they spoke. Maybe he kept them at a girlfriend's house?

She took a sip of her drink, the crisp bubbles tickling her nose. 'I was meaning to ask. How's your bunghole today?'

'Huh?'

'Your bunghole. I do hope you didn't burn it in the shower again.'

It took him a while to understand. Finally he laughed, all his teeth showing. They were off-white but healthy-looking. 'I read that to you, did I?'

How depressing that you could share a joke with someone and they were too drunk to remember it later.

'So how come you've brought the drink this time?'

'He'd be thirty today. He liked a drink.'

'Oh? And what was his tipple if you don't mind me asking?'

'Cider and black.'

'Good choice. That's a quality drink.'

She shrugged. 'Yes, unless it kills you. Like it killed him.'

She watched his brain tick as he processed this. She was keen to see how he'd react.

He went quiet. Took a drink from his flagon.

She'd thought as much.

She had an MP3 player with her. It had belonged to her dead son apparently. She'd been planning, she told him, on putting in some earphones and listening to the music he liked, but after two glasses of Prosecco she decided to hell with it and instead played the songs on loud speaker. They came out tinny but it didn't matter, they decided, because they were awful songs anyway – Pam slapped a hand over her mouth after agreeing with this, as if she'd just blasphemed. Her boy'd had extreme tastes – horrible repetitive metal and bad European pop music. A Eurythmics song came on, and later, a Spandau Ballet number, but apart from these two, it was all noise, harsh noise. She was a respectful lady, Pam – at one point a man who may or may not have been the local postman walked past clutching some yellow flowers, his head down, a cigarette drooping ('Look, it's Humphrey Bogart,' he said), and Pam had paused the music until the man passed out of ear shot. 'If he's Humphrey Bogart then I'm Lauren Bacall,' she said, smirking naughtily, as if saying mean things about people was something she usually tried to suppress.

The Prosecco went fast and Pam got 'tiddly'. She told him about her husband, who was also dead ('Oh, I'm sorry to hear that'). His ashes were buried on the other side of the cemetery and in fact it was his birthday the following week. He'd been a lawyer, a successful one. 'A good man,' she told him. 'Good father, good husband. Didn't see much of him though – he worked such long hours, you see.' It was a heart attack that finished him off. She found him dead behind his steering wheel one morning, the car still in the drive. He'd been working on a case that 'realistically should have gone to a bigger firm.' Too much on his plate.

'See, this is why I bum around,' he said, 'no paperwork, no deadlines, no stress.'

'What about self-respect?' she said.

'I have plenty of self-respect,' he said. 'For example, I will not sleep on dog shit. I have my standards, Pam.'

She laughed, touching his forearm lightly.

It was just as well she hadn't started the Prosecco on an empty stomach – she'd had a full vegetarian breakfast that morning. As it was, she was drunk but not bladdered, unlike Dave. It was the cheap cider he bought, the strong stuff that always had an extra 50% free. She was on the verge of asking him where he got the money from but held her tongue. She'd already got in with a few jabs about the drinking as it was. That's passive aggression, Dennis would have said. He'd gone to AA meetings on two separate occasions; the first time coming back with a whole set of terminology with which to batter her – she was a 'chronic enabler' apparently, and co-dependent and passive aggressive. The second time he'd come back furious, saying everyone there was a self-righteous arsehole – which was rich, she'd thought, coming from him.

It wasn't a good idea to think about this now. It was his birthday. She'd made a deal with herself. The birthdays were for remembering the good times and the anniversary was for dark and maudlin thoughts (a head bent at the wrong angle, one sock halfway off the foot).

'Tell me something interesting about yourself, Dave.'

'There are many interesting things about me, Pamela.'

'Well come on then, let's have it.'

He sat up straighter, clicking his spine –

vertebrae –

'Once, back in the nineties this was, I went on *Stars in Their Eyes*.'

'Oh, shut up.' She'd heard his drunken singing. He was having her on. 'You're having me on.'

'I'm not.' He crossed his heart. 'I promise you I am not.'

'Who were you?'

'Bryan Ferry. I've got some good pipes on me. Well, I used to.'

She still didn't believe him. 'Did you win?'

He shook his head with mock bitterness. 'Stevie Wonder did. A *white* Stevie Wonder! I know you're not supposed to go black-face any more, but *c'mon*.'

'I used to watch that,' she said. 'Dennis too. It was on Saturdays, wasn't it?' She smiled, circling her fingertip around the goblet. 'We used to buy frankfurters and make hot dogs. *Catchphrase*, then *Wheel of Fortune*, then *Blind Date*, then *Stars in Their Eyes*…then I think *Gladiators* came along. Dennis used to love *Gladiators*.' She gave Dave's arm a back-handed slap. 'Mind you, he was probably lusting over those muscle men! And I had no idea.' She hunched over, laughing. 'There we were, eating hot dogs and watching sweaty hunks in spandex…oh, I shouldn't laugh.'

'Gay, was he, your son?'

'Och aye! As they come.'

'Bent as a butcher's, eh?'

'Pardon?'

'Bent as a butcher's hook. That's what my dad used to say. Course, this was back before political correctness.'

She eyed him warily. 'Back in the good old days?'

He raised his hands in protest. 'Hey, I'm all for equal rights! Let's have more gays in the army and let's get the women out of the kitchen.' He drank from his flagon and wiped his chin with the back of his wrist. 'Best place for them, surely, is the bed.' He winked at her and she hit him on the shoulder. 'I thought you were going to behave.'

The song currently playing – a death metal one with those nasty guttural vocals – came to an end. 'Wuthering Heights' by Kate Bush came on.

'Oh, I love this one,' she said. 'Dennis only liked it ironically, or so he said.'

'Ironically?' said Dave.

'Aye. It's very fashionable these days for youngsters to like things ironically.'

Dave stood up. He held out a hand for Pam, silently mouthing the words to the verse. Behind his head the wind gently fluttered the leaves on the trees. She put down her drink and stood up on wobbly legs, taking his hand.

'"It's me-ah, Cathy,"' he sang, wrapping a hand around her waist and waltzing her around the gravestone. She smiled with closed eyes, allowing herself to be led. She could smell cider on his breath, and sensed, rather than saw, flashes of white daylight through her lids. It had been so long since she'd danced with a man. But she was only doing it ironically.

It was the grass tickling his nostrils that woke him up. He lifted his head off the ground. The dead son's – Dennis's – headstone was a few inches from his face. There was the empty Prosecco bottle and two empty flagons. The crotch of his trousers felt cold. Oh, for fucksake. He put his face back down into the grass. He thought of Holly. Oh, Holly. Poor, poor Holly. She hadn't deserved any of it.

He got up and went and sat down cross-legged in front of his own child's grave. She'd slapped him, hadn't she? Pam. Or pushed him? Something like that. Him, reading the signals wrong. Well of course he had! He was a fucking drunk! You drink with drunks and you're going to get groped…or kissed…whatever it was he'd done. The point was, you should accept that the rules will get broken.

Boundaries will get crossed. So it was no good, her acting all high and mighty and getting *disappointed*. What had she thought would happen? That they'd have some beautiful platonic friendship, forged upon the graves of their dead children? Oh, wouldn't that be fucking *nice*?

Stupid bitch.

He put his hands over his eyes. No, that wasn't fair. It wasn't her fault.

He put his hand against the cool stone. Traced a fingertip along the engraved letters. Meaningless. Just lines carved into a stone whereas once there'd been a whole human being, a very small, very whole human being, like a tiny, perfect sun.

May 4th, 2012

Well, thank God for that. He wasn't here. She unfolded her camping chair, sat on it and unzipped her backpack. Only Pringles and Jaffa Cakes this time. She'd save the Prosecco for his 40th.

'Happy birthday, darling boy,' she said.

She hadn't brought flowers. She'd had a good long think about it the night before. Dennis had never given a shite about flowers, unless they were black roses or something Gothic like that.

The weather was mild again this year. It was often the way these days that the spring brought blue skies and warmth and the summer just petered out. Too much cloud, too much rain, heatwaves that lasted only four days. Not like the summers of her youth or her child's youth. She remembered Dennis always playing out the garden with the little girls next door. The older girl would push him around in her doll's pram and their loud laughter was like a host of bushwhacked birds bursting out of foliage. Of course, they'd grown apart,

Dennis and the girls, because they'd gone to a Catholic school and Dennis had gone to the local comprehensive, where he'd made friends with Deena, who would end up, many years later, moving into their street, six houses down. He'd been so excited about that, imagining that their life would be like an episode of *Friends*, the pair of them meeting every day for coffee and popping in each other's houses all the time. But the thing about *Friends* was none of the characters were addicts or alcoholics. Ross and Rachel did not end up pissing the bed after a day of drinking. Phoebe and Joey did not live with their parents. Chandler did not die and Monica did not throw herself out of an attic window.

She took out six Pringles and ate them in two bites, looking around the empty cemetery...no, it was better without him here. All he did was ruin things. She glanced over at his usual spot. A bouquet of white flowers rested against the stone. She got up and took a closer look. They were fresh. Well, that was it – he'd already been. Perhaps the man did feel shame after all. She read the inscription on the stone, taking in the dates. Oh, that wasn't fair. No, that wasn't fair at all. The flowers were carnations as far as she could tell. They looked like they'd come from a supermarket or a petrol station. A bunch of flowers, a couple of bottles of strong cider, some tobacco. But who was she to judge? Who's to say she wouldn't have ended up like him if she were in his shoes?

It was no use thinking about it. The whys, the hows. The man was just another victim of shitty luck and he was probably going to end up here, six feet under with all the other victims, sooner rather than later. And that was none of her business, none at all.

*

Her hand was hot, damp and plump. He laced his fingers through hers and gave a small squeeze. 'He been treating you well?' he said.

She nodded with a soft smile.

'Been taking care of you, has he?'

Another nod. 'He's taken time off work. He's been wonderful.'

She untangled her hand from his and pressed the pain button. She sunk her head back into the pillow. Not a flattering angle. But then he was no prize.

'What does he do again?' he asked.

'He's assistant manager at that sports shop. The big one in town. Can you pass me some water please?'

He grabbed the water jug (his hands were shaking) and poured some into a plastic beaker. He passed it to her and she took a dainty sip.

'What they got you on?' he said.

'Morphine.'

'Ah. The good stuff then.'

She nodded. 'They'll be weaning me off soon though.'

'Will you miss it?' He put his hands on his thighs. Then in his pockets. Then back on his thighs. He wanted a cigarette.

'No. I don't like how it makes me so...fuzzy. You know what I'm like.'

He did. He'd always envied her ambivalence toward intoxication. She could take it or leave it.

'You look well,' he said.

She pulled a face. 'Oh shush, you. I've gotten fat as a house.'

'Just more of you to love,' he said. Then, seeing her face, 'Sorry, I shouldn't have said that. Just an expression, you know.'

'It's OK. You're looking well too. And *I'm* not lying.'

'I've not drunk in six months.'

'Oh, Dave. I'm so glad.' She was such a sincere person, Holly. He could tell that she meant it.

'It's been tough, I won't lie. Especially today.'

She nodded, her eyes closing. Her lids were pale purple.

'Do you ever go visit?' he said. 'I never see you there. I used to look out for you.'

She shook her head. 'I went there once. Remember, that first year? I just…I don't know, Dave. I didn't feel anything. It felt so…I can't think of the right word for it. I go to Roath Park, by where we used to feed the ducks. You remember that bench we always sat on?'

He nodded. 'By the ice cream van.'

'Yes. I've had a plaque put on it.'

'I like the cemetery, me. It's always so peaceful. Until I open my gob.'

They laughed. She spilt some water down her chest. 'Oh flip!' she said, dabbing at the wet spot with a tissue. Her hands were dotted with age spots. She had a white-gold band on her marriage hand. Better than the one he'd got her.

He poured himself a cup of water. It shook in his hand. 'I wanted to apologise, Hol. For the way I was.'

She flapped her hand. 'Don't be silly, Dave. It's been years.'

'No.' He leaned forward and took her hand again. 'I was rotten. I wasn't there for you. It's been weighing on me.'

She looked at him fondly. There were tears in her eyes. 'We've been put through the wringer. Haven't we, da'lin?'

May 4th, 2013

She arrived earlier than usual, so early in fact that she found the custodian unlocking the gates. He was smoking a cigarette, and when he saw her, trudging along with the fold-up camping chair slung over one shoulder, he tried to conceal the cigarette in a cupped hand. As if she was going to grass him up and get him in trouble with Cardiff Council or something!

She made her way through the twisting pathways. It was so unbelievably quiet. It made sense to come early. Not that it was ever busy here. But it was nice knowing that you were the only person in the place, if even for only a few minutes. She stopped to shift the chair to her other shoulder. There was a squirrel perched atop a stone angel. It saw her looking and ran away, weightlessly winding its way up a tree. That could be Dennis in animal form, she thought, before scolding herself. She was always thinking things like that. It was ridiculous. Anyway, if he was going to be any animal it'd be an otter or a skunk (his farts!).

She reached the grave and started to tidy things up – she had some bicarbonate of soda, spirit vinegar, a bottle of water, two rags and some garden scissors. She set to work cleaning the stone and trimming the grass and when that was done, she took out the freshly-cut roses she'd taken from her garden that morning and put them in the flower holder.

'I have decided, with careful consideration, that I like flowers so you're getting bloody flowers. Whether you like it or not.'

She still found, even after five years, that it was an odd, unsettling sensation, her getting the final word on Dennis.

Eight o'clock sharp the garage door began its slow, rattling ascent. He dropped his rollie, stubbing it out with his heel. He could see her bulging court shoes and dumpy ankles surrounded in thick white socks, then her legs, hips, stomach, bosom, neck, chin, and finally her face, which was, as he'd expected, a fucking treat. She was wearing a thick green anorak and had a box of dried cat crunchies in one hand, her walking stick in the other. She raised it in the air, her indignant words drowned out by the still-grinding door. He was surprised she recognised him.

He took a step forward and she reflexively took a step back, her stick, still held aloft, twitching. He laughed and gave her a thumbs-up. Fair enough. He bent down and picked the box of chocolates out of his bag. He stepped forward again, this time very slowly, as if approaching a rattlesnake, and put the chocolates on the ground near her feet, keeping one arm over his head to block any strikes.

'They were my mam's favourite,' he said, stepping back. 'Except the coffee ones. She hated the coffee ones.'

She eyed the box of chocolates warily.

He went back in the rucksack and brought out the other items: six tins of Whiskas cat food; a large sack of dried cat crunchies and a stack of plastic cat food bowls every colour of the rainbow. 'Iams,' he said, lifting the crunchies in the air. 'They're meant to be the best. Look.' He pointed at the label. '"Containing omega fish oils and prebiotics." Makes their fur lovely and glossy.'

'All roight, all roight,' muttered the old woman, like a barely-bemused headmistress who has tolerated this nonsense for long enough. She picked up the box of chocolates and peered at the label, her mouth drawn down. 'Tank you,' she said, begrudgingly.

He bowed deeply, picked his bag off the floor, blew her a kiss and jogged away.

Pam finished the last Jaffa Cake.

'Total eclipse,' she said, through a full mouth. She laughed, putting a hand to her mouth to stop food coming out. 'Well *I* found it funny,' she said to the gravestone. She put a finger in her mouth and scooped the mushed cake from her gums. 'Pardon me.'

'You're pardoned.'

She jumped in her chair, almost falling off. At first she didn't recognise him. His beard was gone for one thing; there was a small white scar on his chin and the old acne pits up his cheeks were deep and ugly. He was wearing glasses. They magnified his eyes and for the first time she noticed the colour of his eyes – they were amber. Instead of the scruffy army coat or the even scruffier leather jacket he was wearing a white shirt with the first two buttons undone. He looked both younger and older.

'Let me guess,' she said. 'You've stopped drinking.'

He nodded. 'A year and half now.' He looked uncomfortable. Of course he did. They always did when they stopped.

He shrugged his rucksack off his shoulder and unzipped it, pulling out a small bunch of flowers, which he held out with a shaking hand. 'For your boy,' he said. She went to take them and at the same time he knelt down and placed them on the grave. Her hand bumped his shoulder and they muttered polite apologies. The silence following went on too long.

'Crisp?' she said, offering the tub of Pringles.

He waved his hand in refusal. 'I'm only eating raw vegetables and seeds these days.'

'Really?'

He smiled. 'Nah.' He put his hands in his pockets. 'I just don't like that flavour.'

'Thank you. For the flowers. That was thoughtful.'

He shrugged, hands still in his pockets. He looked around the graveyard, a light breeze ruffling his shirt collar. Returned his gaze to Pam. 'I can't remember what I did last time I saw you but I have a feeling it was terrible.'

'Aye, it was.'

He nodded. 'Sorry about that. I'm a pig. Well, I was a pig. Maybe I still am.' Another shrug. 'Probably I am. Anyway, sorry.'

'I'm sure I can find it in my heart to forgive you.'

'That means a lot.' He had another look around the graveyard. 'Listen, I want you to do something for me.'

She put the Pringles on the ground. 'What?'

'Close your eyes for me.'

She laughed. 'What? No!'

He put his hands together. 'Please. I swear, it's nothing bad. I won't touch you.'

'Fuck off.'

'I swear on the soul of my dead child that it's nothing bad. Pam? Pamela? Did you hear that? I'm swearing on the immortal soul of my dead fucking child.'

She gave him a look of stern submission, a look she imagined many women before her had given him. He was such a charming little shite, even when struggling with nerves. 'If you *dare* betray my trust…'

He crossed his heart.

She closed her eyes. She heard him going in his bag.

'Keep them closed,' he said. More rummaging. 'One minute. Keep them closed.'

She could hear distant traffic and birds twittering and leaves rustling. She heard him take a long breath, as if gathering himself.

'OK. You can open them.'

He was wearing a black suit jacket over his white shirt and a black tie. He'd swapped his spectacles for black Ray-bans. He had a black wig on. He was holding a microphone. He had a phone or an iPod on the ground, hooked up to small portable speakers. She heard the notes to a familiar song. Roxy Music? Yes, Roxy Music. 'Slave to Love'? Or 'Avalon'? He swayed his hips to the music and smiled wolfishly. Behind him, the wind ruffled the pale grass and the flowers moved as if by themselves. She clapped her hands, laughing with naked delight.

Yes – 'Slave to Love.' His voice was rough and full of cracks, but wonderful. It was wonderful.

ABOUT HONNO

Honno Welsh Women's Press was set up in 1986 by a group of women who felt strongly that women in Wales needed wider opportunities to see their writing in print and to become involved in the publishing process. Our aim is to develop the writing talents of women in Wales, give them new and exciting opportunities to see their work published and often to give them their first 'break' as a writer. Honno is registered as a community co-operative. Any profit that Honno makes is invested in the publishing programme. Women from Wales and around the world have expressed their support for Honno. Each supporter has a vote at the Annual General Meeting. For more information and to buy our publications, please write to Honno at the address below, or visit our website: www.honno.co.uk

Honno, 14 Creative Units, Aberystwyth Arts Centre, Aberystwyth, Ceredigion SY23 3GL

Honno Friends

We are very grateful for the support
of the Honno Friends:
Jane Aaron, Gwyneth Tyson Roberts, Beryl Thomas

For more information on how you can support Honno, see:
https://www.honno.co.uk/about/support-honno/